W9-BCR-411

FIC
CHR

C_1

Christopher,

Dive right in.

$15.95

34880030015312

DATE			

DIVE RIGHT IN

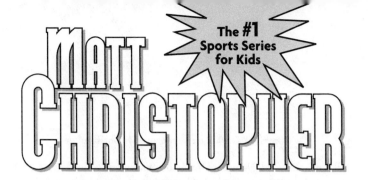

The #1
Sports Series
for Kids

DIVE RIGHT IN

Text by Robert Hirschfeld

Little, Brown and Company
Boston   New York   London

Copyright © 2002 by Catherine M. Christopher

First Edition

Matt Christopher™ is a trademark of Catherine M. Christopher.

Text by Robert Hirschfeld

Library of Congress Cataloging-in-Publication Data

Christopher, Matt.
    Dive right in / Matt Christopher ; text by Robert Hirschfeld. — 1st ed.
       p. cm.
    "The #1 sports series for kids."
    Summary: Forced to quit gymnastics to avoid serious injury, twelve-year-old Traci tries to fill the void in her life by taking up diving.
    ISBN 0-316-34919-4 (hc) / ISBN 0-316-34921-6 (pb)
    [1. Diving — Fiction.   I. Hirschfeld, Robert, 1942– . II. Title.
PZ7.C458 Dlk   2002
[Fic] — dc21   2001042281

10 9 8 7 6 5 4 3 2 1

MV-NY

Printed in the United States of America

DIVE RIGHT IN

Traci Winchell stood motionless on the balance beam, four feet above the mat-covered gym floor. Gracefully, she bent forward, laid her hands on the beam, and kicked up into a handstand. She held it a few seconds before slowly lowering her feet to the beam again.

Traci prepared for her dismount, a series of moves including a cartwheel, a flip, and a forward somersault off the beam. If she did it right, she would land on her feet, motionless.

She didn't do it right. The cartwheel was okay, but Traci's balance went off in the flip. When she hit the mat, she stumbled forward a few steps. Worse, she felt sharp pain in her knees from the force of the landing. Her knees had been giving her trouble recently. She flexed each in turn, scowling.

For many people, just walking on a balance beam without falling would be a challenge. For twelve-year-old Traci, it was as easy as walking on a sidewalk. She had been taking gymnastics classes since she was four. She was good in all the other events in girls' gymnastics — vault, floor exercise, uneven parallel bars — but the balance beam was her favorite. Lately, however, she was having trouble and wasn't sure why.

As she bent to examine her knees, Traci noticed a stranger in the gym, a tall woman with graying blond hair, walking toward her. The woman seemed to be studying her. Traci straightened up.

"Your knees are bothering you." The woman spoke in a matter-of-fact way, without any introduction. "Have you thought about whether gymnastics is really your sport?"

"What?" Traci couldn't believe her ears. "What are you talking about?"

The woman didn't smile, nor did she give a clue as to who she was or what she was doing there. Traci was pretty sure she wasn't anyone's mom, because she'd met all the moms.

The woman said, "I bet you've grown at least three inches in the last year. And put on a lot of weight — mostly muscle."

Traci blinked. The woman was right about that. Traci had grown *four* inches, and, while she was still thin, she'd added a good deal of muscle, especially in her arms and legs.

The woman turned and gestured to the other girls in the gym. "Look around," she said. "You're the tallest, heaviest girl here. You must have noticed. I'll bet that some girls who weren't as good as you have caught up, maybe gotten better. Like the one who did that vault."

The woman pointed to a slender, dark-haired girl who happened to be Traci's best friend, Valerie Ling. Valerie was the most gifted athlete in class. Because she lived near Traci, the two girls spent a lot of time together.

"The reason your knees are giving you trouble," the woman went on before Traci could think of anything to say, "is that gymnastics is a high-impact sport. It's rough on the knees and ankles. It could get worse, especially if you grow more. Your joints *and* your gymnastic performance are likely to get worse. You should think about that before real problems develop."

Traci finally found her voice. "Is that so? What should I do, then? Quit? Give up on being an athlete? Is that what you think?"

The woman shook her head. "Not at all. I think you should think about giving up *this* sport and try a new one."

"Oh, really?" Traci said, not bothering to keep some sarcasm out of her voice.

The woman didn't react. "I was thinking of diving," she said. "Diving doesn't put as much strain on the knees and ankles. And the same athletic skills that made you a promising gymnast — balance, coordination, and strength — will also help to make you a very good diver, if you're willing to work hard at it."

"Diving," Traci repeated. "You think I should try diving."

"I do," the woman replied. "I happen to coach divers, and I know talent when I see it. You're a good prospect, which is why I'm here."

"Trace?" Traci's gymnastics coach, Jeff, was hurrying over. Traci loved Jeff and had worked in his classes for four years. He was a nice, easygoing guy who always had an encouraging word for his students. "I see you two have already met."

Traci looked from the woman to her coach. "You know her?" she asked him.

"Sure do," said Jeff with a smile. "This is Margo Armstead." He paused, as if expecting Traci to react to the name. But it meant nothing to her. "Margo's a great diving coach. When she heard about you, she was eager to meet you. So I invited her to come."

"She heard about me?" Traci repeated. "From who?"

"I have to go to my own classes now," said Margo, reaching into a canvas tote bag she was carrying. "Traci, I think you might have the makings of a good diver, if you want to be. Please think about it and let me know whether you are interested. Here's my number." She pulled a card from the bag and gave it to Traci. With a nod to Jeff, she turned and walked away.

Traci stared after her and then looked at Jeff. The

coach looked unhappy, as if he'd been caught doing something he shouldn't have done. "Jeff, did you tell that woman about me?"

Jeff took a deep breath. "Her name is Margo Armstead. Yes, I told her about you."

Valerie Ling came hurrying over, but slowed down as she sensed that Jeff and Traci were having a serious talk.

"Why?" asked Traci.

"I thought it would be a good idea."

"Why?" Traci asked again. "Is what she said true? About me, I mean."

"Trace?" Valerie said. "Something wrong?"

Traci didn't answer Valerie; she kept her attention focused on the coach. "That woman said —"

"Her name is *Margo,*" said Jeff.

Traci shrugged. "*Margo* said because I grew so much I'll never be a top gymnast. I'll mess up my knees and I won't get any better."

Jeff held up a hand. "She didn't say that you would never get any better."

"You know what I mean," Traci snapped, feeling a little panicky. Gymnastics had been the most important thing in her life for almost as long as she could remember. "Is what she says right? Is that why you told her about me, because I'll never be a top gymnast? Do you want me out?"

"Trace, you're welcome to stay in my class as long as you want," the coach assured her. "You know I'd never kick you out."

"But is Margo *right*?" Traci repeated. "That's what I want to know."

Jeff sighed. "Well . . . okay. I've been putting this off for a while, but it isn't fair to you not to talk about it."

Traci felt her panic rise higher. "Talk about what?"

"What's going on?" asked Valerie, looking worried for her friend.

Jeff looked at Traci steadily. "You *have* grown a lot this past year. You're the tallest girl here by three inches. And you're heavier. Once, this wouldn't be a drawback. Years ago, many top gymnasts were big. But now . . . you see world-class competition on TV, Trace. They're almost all slender and not tall."

"What are you telling me?" asked Traci, unable to keep her voice from trembling.

Jeff looked distressed. "Trace, you want a shot at the top. That won't happen for you in gymnastics."

Traci felt her eyes begin to tear.

"That's why I called Margo," Jeff went on. "You have the skills and attitude of a great athlete. But, if you want to excel, gymnastics isn't for you. Not anymore."

This isn't happening, Traci thought, her stomach churning.

"Margo is a great coach," Jeff went on. "She's coached a few Olympic medalists. She didn't say that you might be a good diver to make you feel good. Margo always says what she thinks. If you want to keep working with me, that's fine, but you should know that your prospects are limited. And Margo's right about you risking serious knee problems down the line as a gymnast."

Valerie squeezed Traci's hand as Traci fought back tears.

"Anyway," said Jeff, "think it over, okay? If you want to talk, I'm available."

Traci spent the rest of practice in a daze. Later, she walked home with Valerie. Neither girl spoke at first. Traci didn't feel up to it. Finally, Valerie broke the silence.

"You probably won't see it this way, but this could

be a good thing. Margo is obviously a hot coach. I mean, she's worked with Olympic *medalists!* Maybe you should call her."

Traci stared at Valerie. "But I'm a gymnast!" She couldn't believe her best friend was betraying her like this.

"What if you wreck your knees?" Valerie's face was pinched with concern.

Traci shook her head. "I don't know. Margo was *cold.* I didn't like her."

Valerie turned as they reached her gate. "Well, I'll see you. And you should think about it. I'd love to have a coach who's worked with Olympic medalists."

The girls hugged, and Traci headed for home. *No way!* she thought to herself. *I couldn't be a diver.*

But another voice in her head said, *You sure about that?*

2

Traci usually ate a big dinner, but this evening she pushed the food around on her plate.

"Sweetie, are you feeling all right?" Mrs. Winchell asked.

Traci nodded. "Yeah, I guess."

"When you don't eat, something's wrong," Mr. Winchell said. "What is it?"

Traci explained what had happened in gymnastics class. Her mother looked sympathetic. "We know what this means to you, but if there's a risk of permanent knee damage, then it's a good thing your coach spoke up."

"What's the diving coach's name?" asked Pete, Traci's sixteen-year-old brother.

Traci made a sour face. "Margo Armstead," she said.

Pete laughed. "I was going to ask what she's like, but from the look on your face, I already have an idea. Not your kind of person, huh?"

Traci sighed. "She was totally cold. She said, 'You'll never be a gymnast, and you'll mess up your knees' like she was talking about the weather. Zero sympathy."

"Will you call her?" asked Traci's father.

Traci had thought of little else since getting home, but she still didn't have an answer. "I don't know what to do," she said at last. "I've never dived off a board in my life. I don't know if I could be a diver, and I don't know if I can work with this Margo, either."

Mr. Winchell put a hand on Traci's shoulder. "Honey, your mom and I are always there if you want to talk about these things, but this decision is really yours to make. Whatever you finally decide to do, we're behind you all the way. I hope you know that."

A little later, Traci was sitting alone in the den when Pete looked in. "Want company, or should I stay out?"

Traci gave her brother a weak smile. "Come on in. It's okay."

Pete didn't love athletics the way Traci did. He worked on his school newspaper, and his great ambition was to be a successful writer.

"Guess you feel pretty bad," said Pete.

Traci stared at the rug under her feet. "I've been doing gymnastics forever. I'm good at it. Now, all of a sudden it's all over for me — because I'm too *tall?* It's not fair!"

Pete nodded. "Hey, you won't get an argument from me. But it could be worse. What if you really did blow out a knee?"

"Yeah, I guess. But that doesn't mean I have to feel happy about it," Traci answered.

"But there *is* something you can feel happy about," Pete said. "It isn't as if you're all through as an athlete. You can still do it. What's more, there's a coach, a very good coach, who thinks you have what it takes. I think you should give it a shot. You can always change your mind later."

Traci smiled at Pete. "Thanks. I think I'll call Valerie and talk to her about it."

She made the call from her bedroom.

"How are you doing?" Valerie asked. "Did you call that coach?"

"Not yet," Traci said. "I thought I'd talk to you first."

"Sure," said Valerie. "Well, you already know what I think. I think you should call her, before she changes her mind."

Traci sighed. "Pete says the same thing."

"He's right. Why wouldn't you want to?" Valerie asked. "If it was me, I'd jump at the chance to work with a coach like that."

Traci snorted. "If Jeff told you you'd never be a first-class gymnast, you'd just say, 'Oh well,' and go on from there? I don't *think* so."

There was a pause on Valerie's end. "Well, I guess I'd be depressed about it, sure. But even if I felt bad, I'd call that coach. Just like I think you will. You're as ambitious as I am. You know you're good, and you aren't going to let it all go without a fight."

"But you think Jeff was right?" Traci asked. "About me being too tall for gymnastics?"

Traci could hear Valerie sigh over the phone. "I hate to say it, but yeah. I mean, it's true, all the best ones *are* built like me. And it's true that you've been having more trouble lately, even on the beam — your specialty.

"And another thing," Valerie continued before Traci could say anything. "If I hurt a knee or an ankle so that I could never compete in any sport again, I don't know what I'd do. That would truly be the worst. It's hard to imagine quitting gymnastics, but the idea of having to give up sports totally . . ."

Valerie trailed off without finishing, but Traci knew what her friend meant. Maybe she *was* lucky, at that. "Okay, thanks. I guess I'll call Margo."

"Great!" Valerie exclaimed. "It's the right thing for you to do. I mean, it'll be the pits not having you in class anymore, but it's not like we won't see each other. After all, you're still my best friend."

After Traci hung up, she found the coach's card and made the phone call before she changed her mind.

The coach answered right away. "Yes?"

Traci winced a little at the flat, cool voice, but plowed ahead. "Uh, this is Traci Winchell. From this afternoon?"

"Yes?" said the coach again.

"I was thinking and . . . I want to try it, if it's still all right with you. Diving, I mean."

"All right. Get a pencil and paper." Margo gave

Traci an address and a list of equipment to bring along. "Please be ready tomorrow afternoon at four."

Traci was about to say something about how she appreciated the opportunity and was looking forward to it, but before she could say it, Margo said, "Good-bye," and hung up.

Wonderful, Traci thought, looking at the phone in her hand. *This should be a lot of fun.*

3

Traci was ten minutes early for her meeting with Margo. To her surprise, the place wasn't a specialized diving center, but an ordinary health club like the one her parents used. Through glass doors at the back of the lobby, Traci saw a swimming pool but no diving board. It wasn't what she had expected.

Margo came through another set of doors, looking at her watch impatiently despite the fact that Traci was early.

"Hello," she said, with the total lack of warmth that Traci was learning to expect from her. "Put on your suit and meet me by the pool with your gear."

As she changed, Traci realized that she was rushing, though she wasn't late. However, she wanted to make a good impression, and rushing seemed like a smart choice. She ran to meet the coach by the pool, carrying the gym bag with the things Margo had told her to bring.

"Let's see your gear," said the coach. Traci opened the bag, and Margo, after a quick check, gave Traci a jerky nod. By Margo's standards, it felt like high praise.

Traci held up a piece of soft, heavy cloth the size of a large handkerchief. Mrs. Winchell had picked it up at a sports store that morning. The package it came in read "chamois"; Margo had pronounced it "shammy." It looked and felt like something Mr. Winchell used to wash the car. "What's this for?" Traci asked.

"To dry off after dives," Margo said. "Come here to the pool. Can you swim?"

Traci couldn't help staring at the coach. Could she *swim?* When Traci failed to answer immediately, Margo snapped, "Don't you know whether you swim or not?"

Despite wanting to make a good impression, Traci was irritated. "Sure, I can swim," she said, knowing she sounded annoyed.

"Good," Margo replied. If she sensed Traci's annoyance, she didn't show it. "Not everyone can swim,

17

you know. Please get in and swim the length of the pool and back."

Traci was puzzled, but jumped in. A fair swimmer, Traci swam to the shallow end of the pool and back — twenty-five yards each way.

Margo nodded again. "Now, swim underwater as far as you can."

Traci went slightly more than half the length of the pool before needing air, about fifteen yards. Not bad, she thought. Margo said nothing, so it was apparently okay with her, too.

Margo had Traci demonstrate a few other basic skills. At the coach's direction, Traci swam down to touch the bottom of the pool at its greatest depth, then did it again, this time picking up a coin that the coach had thrown into the water. Traci went across the pool, using only leg kicks while holding a kickboard. She was surprised at how hard it was and how long it took.

"Good," Margo said. Traci wondered if she'd actually get to dive, now that she had proven that she wouldn't drown in a swimming pool.

Not just yet. Instead, Margo said, "Please come here," and pointed to the side of the pool. Following

Margo's instructions, Traci knelt on one knee at the edge of the pool.

"Good," said Margo. "Now, roll forward into the pool, tucking your chin in and extending your arms before you hit the water. Once you hit the water, flex your hands so your fingers point up toward the surface."

Traci nodded and executed the move, straightening her arms so her hands cut the surface of the water before her head went in.

When she surfaced, Margo beckoned her out of the pool. "Your chin wasn't tucked in enough. Also, you didn't extend your hands properly when they hit the water, and you didn't point your fingers up. Once again. This time, tuck your chin in tightly and try to control your hands more carefully."

Traci didn't have a clue what this proved, but tried to follow Margo's instructions in every detail.

"Better," Margo said, though she wasn't completely happy. "Once again. Time the extension of your hands so that your fingers are straight just before they reach the surface of the water — not too long before and not after."

Good grief! Traci thought but didn't say. She did it

again . . . and again. Finally, Margo said, "Enough. Now, stand at the edge of the pool and bend slowly forward from the waist — keep your legs straight — until you fall forward toward the water. Then, tuck in your chin and straighten your arms and hands as before."

Traci ran through the instructions in her head and nodded. Then she did what Margo had told her, or so she thought. But Margo had Traci repeat the move several times, making tiny corrections each time. Once it was the position of her shoulders before she started forward; once Margo thought that Traci's head wasn't exactly aligned with her spine, so she used her hands to make a slight adjustment in Traci's posture. Finally, Margo was satisfied.

Traci couldn't resist asking, "What was I doing just then?"

"That was what we call the 'pike position,'" Margo replied. "When you do a dive where you bend at the waist but your legs are straight, that is the pike position. As you approach the water, you straighten out — that's the 'come-out.' Then you enter the water with your body in a straight line and with as little splash as possible. The other diving positions are called the 'tuck' and 'straight' positions."

Margo paused while Traci dried herself with the chamois. "In the tuck, you tuck your body into a tight ball and do a come-out before you hit the water, just like you do from the pike position. When you went into the water after kneeling, you were basically doing the tuck position. In a dive done from the straight position, your body remains in a straight line. Is this clear?"

Traci nodded.

"Good," Margo said. "There are many dives from each position. In some, you go off the board or platform facing toward the pool. In others, your back is to the pool. Some dives require somersaults. Others involve twisting your body. Those are harder. But don't worry about all that. We have a lot of basics to do. Let's get back to work."

This time, Traci dove from the edge of the pool without bending at all — the straight position. Margo frowned.

"What you did just then would have been fine if you were swimming in a race. You jumped *forward,* as if you wanted to cover as much distance as possible before you hit the water. That's the right idea, for a racer. But a diver needs to jump *up*, to get the height you need to execute a dive before entering the water. Try again — and think about jumping *up* instead of *out*."

Traci thought for a moment and tried to jump higher. It felt odd, and, as she climbed out of the pool, she said so.

"It will feel normal eventually," Margo said. Traci did several more, trying to adjust according to Margo's constant and (Traci thought) picky correction. She knew she'd done well when Margo said nothing. Apparently, unlike Jeff, this coach didn't believe in praise.

Finally, Margo said, "Please change into the workout clothes you brought. I'll meet you in the second-floor exercise room."

Traci changed in the locker room, used a neat little machine that dried out her swimsuit in a few seconds, then went upstairs. The exercise room contained several mats and a large, round trampoline. Traci felt more at home there.

Margo was waiting, looking impatient again. Traci

suspected that Margo *always* looked that way. With Margo was another woman, younger, with curly brown hair and a warm smile.

Margo gestured to the other woman. "This is my assistant, Sophia Brigati. You'll be spending a lot of time with her, especially at first, if you continue in my program."

"Hi, Traci," Sophia said. "I'm looking forward to working with you."

"With your gymnastic background, I assume you've spent time on trampolines," Margo said. Obviously, chat time was over.

Traci nodded. "Sure. We have one — *had* one — just like this for Jeff's class."

"I think we can work without the safety harness, then. Sophia will help spot you," said Margo.

As Traci knew, "spotters" watched while athletes worked on equipment where accidents might happen. An experienced spotter could almost always keep the athlete from getting a serious injury.

Traci swung onto the trampoline and did some warm-up jumps, getting used to its surface and tautness. Then, following Margo's direction, she went through some simple acrobatics: forward and back somersaults and flips. Margo had Traci do front and back flips in the pike position — with straight legs, bending only at the waist. After the constant correction at the pool, Margo had little to say here. It was obvious that gymnastics had been good training for some aspects of diving.

Margo then had Traci do some of the same moves on a mat. There, too, she had nothing to say. Traci noticed that Margo and Sophia were making comments to each other that she couldn't hear.

After ten minutes of work on the mat, Sophia said, "See you soon," waved, and left. Margo turned to Traci. "Please meet me here on Saturday morning at ten o'clock."

Surprised, Traci asked, "We're done for today? Am I going to dive Saturday?"

"Not until you're ready," Margo replied. "Remember, you're getting a late start and there is still much to learn."

She nodded and walked away. Traci watched her go, wondering if she should feel happy or annoyed.

So, do you like diving? How was the new coach?" asked Pete, as he grabbed a drumstick from the chicken platter.

Traci frowned. "I don't know. Margo isn't exactly Miss Personality. We were there for two hours, and she never said a single nice word. She just kept giving me these really fussy little criticisms. And I never got to dive."

"If you never got to dive," Mr. Winchell said, "what was the coach correcting?"

Traci explained what she had done in the pool and in the exercise room. "It was really kind of dull, not at all what I was expecting."

Mrs. Winchell said, "It sounds to me like this coach wanted to see what you could do, and how you responded to corrections. She doesn't know you, after all, and she's right: You *are* new to diving, and you're a late starter."

"Margo sounds like my English teacher this year," said Pete. "She can really be brutal to me and a couple of others in the class. Most of the kids she doesn't treat that way, but with a few of us . . ." He shook his head.

"At first I thought she was picking on me because she didn't like me for some reason," Pete continued. "But then I decided it isn't that at all. She wants me to do well, and this is her way of getting me to work harder. And the fact is that I *am* working harder, and writing better."

"Seems to me that it's way too early to pass judgment on this Margo," Traci's father said. "Let's see what happens over time, and maybe she'll lighten up, or you'll get used to it, or you'll see it as a challenge, like Pete and his English teacher. And, Trace, nobody's forcing you to go on with this. You can always quit."

When Traci left the dinner table, she felt a little annoyed. Her family hadn't been as sympathetic as they should have been. And there was no way she was going to quit — not yet, anyway.

She was doing her homework when there was a knock on the door of her room. Traci opened it to see Valerie holding her gym bag.

"I had to stop by and see how it was," said Valerie, tossing her bag on Traci's floor and flopping onto the bed. "How do you like her? Was she totally awful?"

"Not *totally* awful," Traci said, "but I didn't like her. She's really cold, and nothing pleases her. She had me doing this really boring stuff over and over, and she made a million tiny little corrections. 'Once again, and hold your left shoulder a millionth of an inch higher than your right shoulder. . . . Once again, and flex your wrists a teensy bit less. . . . Once again. . . . Once again. . . .' It was making me crazy."

"Huh," Valerie said. "So you hated it."

Traci sighed. "Jeff was always giving you compliments. Even when you messed up, he'd say something to make you feel better. He's really sweet, you know? And Margo is just so . . . icy. Working with her isn't going to be any fun at all. Zero."

Valerie nodded, looking thoughtful. "I see what you mean. But maybe it'll be better when you're in a group, working with other girls. There'll be people you can talk to, and that should help."

"Maybe," Traci agreed. "If she lets you talk, that is. She may not let you talk or think about anything but diving and keeping your hands flexed. It wouldn't surprise me if she ran things like a prison."

Valerie laughed. "Wow. You really don't like her, do you?"

Traci shrugged, irritated. "What's to like?"

"I see what you mean," said Valerie, "but I wonder: Is being nice and sweet what you want in a coach? Don't forget, Margo has trained athletes who won Olympic medals. She must have *something* going for her to do that."

"You can be a great coach and still be nice," Traci pointed out.

"I wonder," said Valerie. She started picking at Traci's bedspread. "I mean, I agree that Jeff is a very nice guy. But how many champions has *he* trained? Has he worked with any Olympic medalists?"

"Who knows?" Traci replied. "For all we know, he's worked with top gymnasts."

Valerie raised her eyebrows. "Oh, come on, Trace. If Jeff had worked with champions, you really think we wouldn't have heard about it in all these years? You think he'd have kept it a secret? I don't believe it!"

Traci stared at Valerie. "It sounds to me like you aren't so crazy about Jeff. Is that true?"

Valerie lowered her gaze and started picking at the spread again. She didn't say anything for several seconds.

"Val? What is it?" Traci prodded.

Finally, Valerie looked up. "Don't spread this around, but I've been thinking about finding a new coach."

Traci's eyes opened wide. *"Really?"*

Valerie nodded. "I talked about it with my parents, and we have a few names we're checking out. But I don't want Jeff to know, unless we're actually going to make the switch."

"That's amazing," Traci said.

"Not really," said Valerie. "You know that I want to be a top gymnast. And if it takes some kind of hard-nosed type to get me there . . . well, then that's what I want. Athletes who win gold medals, or even silver or bronze medals, aren't in it just for fun."

"When you put it like that," Traci admitted, "it makes sense. But I really loved working with Jeff. I think it would be hard to walk out on him, at least for me."

Valerie shrugged. "I don't believe that. I think you're as ambitious as I am, and that you'd have done what I'm doing, sooner or later. See, Trace, I think you caught a lucky break. I think the best thing Jeff ever did for you was to call Margo."

When Traci didn't answer, Valerie pressed her point.

"Here's the way I see it. If you want to have a shot at being the best, you have to do whatever it takes. Maybe you can have fun and maybe you can't, but 'fun' isn't what matters. You need to work with someone who will make you work hard, force you to make the most of your talent. From what you've said, Margo is that kind of coach. That's the kind of coach I want for myself."

She laid her hand on her friend's arm. "I'm ready to pay the price. You ought to decide if you are, too. Think about what you really want."

Valerie left a few minutes later. As Traci closed her bedroom door, she couldn't stop thinking about what Valerie had said.

What did she really want?

5

Traci arrived at the pool fifteen minutes early Saturday morning. Her second session was a lot like her first, though Margo actually did have Traci do some diving — but only from the edge of the pool. She said Traci needed to work on getting more elevation, more upward movement.

"I thought a springboard would do that for me," Traci said at one point.

"You need to do it for yourself, too," Margo replied. "Also, when you dive from a platform, there is no spring involved."

Margo added one new item to Traci's limited repertoire: a forward dive in the pike position. As usual, Margo had a thousand little corrections for Traci to remember as she did the dive over and over. But, even though she found the repetition boring,

Traci realized that it helped her become more natural in movements that were new to her.

When Sophia arrived, she took Traci to do some more work on the mats and the trampoline. At the end of the session, Margo gave Traci a piece of paper with an address written down on it.

"This is where you will be training from now on. Be there on Tuesday at four."

"Is that the place where your divers work out?" Traci asked.

Margo gave one of her stiff nods. "You will be joining one of the groups on Tuesday. You'll be working mostly with Sophia. I will come in to observe from time to time."

Traci was surprised to discover she was a little disappointed that she'd be working with Margo's assistant rather than Margo herself. But she comforted herself with the knowledge that Sophia was a nice woman who actually smiled and was willing to give out a compliment now and then.

When Traci arrived for her session on Tuesday, she looked around her, thinking that this was more like it. There were three big pools. The first two had diving boards of different heights, from one meter, or just over three feet, above the pool, to three meters — almost ten feet — from the water. The three-meter boards made Traci nervous; they seemed uncomfortably high.

When she looked at the diving platforms at the third pool, she felt dizzy. The three platforms were attached to an enormous tower, with a staircase that went to the top. The lowest platform, which jutted out from the left side of the tower, was three meters above the water. The next platform, projecting from the right side of the tower, was five meters up. The highest tower, jutting from the middle of the tower, was *ten* meters up. Ten meters was over thirty feet. Diving off a ten-meter platform would be like diving off the roof of a three-story building! Traci wondered how anyone ever had the nerve to do that. She doubted that she could ever get herself to dive from up there, even for an Olympic gold medal.

"Traci! Welcome!" Sophia came over, smiling. "Ready to go to work?"

Traci liked Sophia's attitude a lot more than Margo's. She smiled back and answered, "Absolutely!"

"I'll take you to the locker room and assign you a

locker," Sophia said. "Then you can get into workout clothes and meet us in the workout room. Okay?"

"Not the pool?" Traci had hoped to do some diving today.

Sophia's smile became apologetic. "Not today. We're going to start with some introductory stuff. I'm afraid you won't be getting wet just yet."

Traci hid her disappointment, reminding herself not to be impatient. She changed, then headed for the exercise room. This was a large, brightly lit space with mats, a couple of trampolines, and bare floor, some of which was marked out in mysterious patterns.

Sophia was there, along with about a dozen girls, who seemed to be between seven and nine years old.

"Come on over," Sophia called. "Meet the other girls."

The other girls? thought Traci. *Is* this *the group I'll be working with?*

The girls were talking among themselves and eyeing Traci with curiosity. Sophia said, "Girls, this is Traci, a new student here. She'll be working with us for a while."

Stunned, Traci barely managed to smile and say, "Hello."

There was a chorus of hello's and hi's from the young girls, along with a few giggles. Sophia must have seen Traci's confusion. She said, "Listen, girls, you get started on your warm-ups. I'm going to show Traci around."

Sophia gestured for Traci to go with her. The two walked across the room, where they could speak without being overheard.

"Uh . . ." Traci wasn't sure what she wanted to say. "I was . . . I sort of thought . . . aren't there girls here who are my age?"

"Not at the moment," Sophia said. "I mean, Margo works with girls of various ages. But the girls of your age or older who work with Margo are experienced divers. The only ones who are relatively new to diving are the younger ones, like these girls here. Actually, even *they* have some experience. I can see why it feels strange, but until you've got a foundation, you're not ready to work with girls of your own age. You'll get used to it, and it won't be forever. All right?"

It *wasn't* all right, but Traci had to admit that

Sophia was making sense. Traci was a beginner, and she'd have to stick it out with these little kids — at least for now.

"Okay," Traci said. "I know I'm new at this."

"That's the right way to look at it," Sophia said. "Let's get going."

The class started out with ten minutes of stretching. This was standard routine for Traci: Keeping joints flexible was just as necessary for a gymnast as it was for a diver. The little girls were as supple as the gymnasts Traci had worked with.

The group then went on to do a forty-minute calisthenic routine that left Traci breathing hard. Most of the younger girls, Traci was surprised to see, seemed to be in better shape than she was.

Traci wasn't sure whether this meant that divers generally needed to be stronger, or that Margo believed in working her people harder than Jeff had done. She suspected that Jeff had been more easygoing, and wondered if this was a point for Jeff — or against him. Traci remembered what Valerie had said about choosing between having fun and paying the price to get what you wanted.

Traci couldn't help noticing a few of the girls staring at her and whispering together. There was even a little giggling, although Sophia quickly put a stop to it and spoke sharply to the girls involved.

Traci gritted her teeth. She could understand that the presence of an older, bigger girl in this group would appear weird to these kids. At their age, she might have been one of the gigglers herself. Still, it bothered her. She resolved to work as hard as she could so she could graduate to kids her own age.

After the workout, some girls went to work in a pool, while others practiced tumbling on the mats. A few high-school-aged girls helped, spotting for the young girls.

Sophia called Traci over to a corner of the exercise room. In her hand she had a tape measure.

"Who are those older girls?" asked Traci.

"They're some of Margo's divers. They sometimes help out with this class. I need to take a few measurements of you."

"For what?" Traci asked.

"You'll see in a minute," Sophia said, kneeling next to Traci. She measured both of Traci's legs from knee to floor, and then measured the length of her feet. She jotted down the measurements on a sheet of paper. She did some arithmetic with a calculator and wrote down the results on the paper.

As she wrote, Sophia said, "Thanks to gymnastics, there are some things you won't have to work on. Your posture is already excellent, for one thing. A lot of girls just starting out don't know how to stand. You do. But you're going to have to spend a lot of time on your approach and hurdle."

Traci's face must have showed that she had no idea what Sophia meant. Sophia smiled and wrote more things on another piece of paper. When she was done, she showed the paper to Traci. On it was a line drawing of a long, oblong shape.

"That's a drawing of a diving board," Sophia explained. "When you do a forward dive off a board, you start from a position toward the back of the board and take a few steps toward the end. That's called the 'approach.' Then you take a kind of hop off one leg — that's what we call the 'hurdle.' You come down on both feet, flex at the knees, and take off into the dive."

"How many steps?" asked Traci.

"It depends," said Sophia. "First, you'll decide which is your 'drive leg' — the one you jump off for the hurdle — and which is the 'hurdle leg' — the one you swing upward in the hurdle. Then you'll figure out whether you feel more comfortable making the first step of your approach with your left or right leg.

"Let's say you start your approach with your left leg and your drive leg is also your left leg. Then your approach will be four steps: left, right, left, right, drive with your left — and into the hurdle. Which leg will you feel more comfortable driving off for the hurdle?"

After walking through some imitation approaches and hurdles, Traci decided that she felt better driving off her right leg and that she also liked starting her approach with her right leg.

"Okay, then you'll use a four-step approach," said Sophia, marking some lines on the paper outline of the diving board. "These lines show you where your toes should be after each step of your approach. It's based on the length of your leg and of your foot — the measurements I just took. And notice that the last step — the one that leads into the hurdle — should be longer than the first three steps, by about one third."

"*Wow!*" Traci said, looking at the paper. "It has to be that exact?" She looked at Sophia, wondering if this precision might be a joke.

Sophia didn't smile. "Yes, it has to be that exact." She pointed to a painted outline on the floor. "That's the outline of a diving board. I'm going to tape off the four steps of your approach here so you can start practicing. You'll need to make an outline like this somewhere at home and tape off the steps on it, using these measurements. Then you can practice that approach over and over, until you can do it in your sleep."

Traci watched Sophia measure and tape lines on the floor. "I never realized that it had to be so precise."

Sophia looked up at Traci. "Believe me, it does. Margo may seem picky to you right now, but that's one reason she's such a good coach. She insists on perfection. Did you ever hear the expression 'Practice makes perfect'?"

"Sure," Traci replied. "That's what Margo thinks, huh?"

Sophia shook her head. "Margo's version is a little different. She says, '*Perfect* practice makes perfect.' And she's right. You can't be casual in diving. What may seem like tiny mistakes can lead to really bad results. So find a space, draw the outline, and measure the lines for the steps. *Exactly* like it is here. If you can do it where you can watch yourself in a mirror, that would be even better."

"Okay, I'll do it tonight," Traci said. She was beginning to understand the difference between what she'd been doing with Jeff and the demands of a coach like Margo.

"The other thing you need to work on," Sophia said, "is learning how to jump."

"I already know how to jump," Traci protested. "Watch."

She bent her knees and jumped.

"See?"

Sophia sighed. "That's what I mean. That's not how divers jump. You swung your arms up as your legs pushed you up."

"That's wrong?" asked Traci, startled.

Sophia explained, "Divers swing their arms up *before* they push off on their legs. Try doing it."

Traci tried, but it took her three attempts to get the synchronization. "Wow," she said. "That feels totally wrong."

Sophia grinned. "That's why you have to work on it. You need to get to the point where it feels totally *right*. You have a few old habits to unlearn, and that's one of them."

"I guess I do," Traci admitted. "Sounds like I have a long way to go."

Sophia nodded. "That's what I've been trying to tell you. But you can do it. Other people have made the same transition from gymnastics to diving. You have the skill. The question is whether or not you have the *will*."

Suddenly, Traci felt that she was on familiar ground. She was facing a challenge. She knew about challenges, and in the past she'd managed to meet them successfully. That was what competition was all about.

She grinned back at Sophia. "I have that, too. I'll do whatever it takes."

"I have a feeling you will," Sophia agreed. "I think you should start drilling yourself on the approach, the hurdle, and the diver's jump. Okay?"

Traci took a deep breath. "Okay," she said.

6

When Traci arrived for the next workout, Sophia asked, "Have you been working on the approach and hurdle?"

"I spent hours on it," Traci said. "I may not do it in my sleep yet, but pretty nearly."

"I'm not surprised," Sophia said. "And I have good news for you. After warm-ups in the exercise room, you'll do some work in a pool."

"Really?" Traci beamed happily. "You mean I'll be diving? Off a board?"

Sophia held up a hand. "Not today. But you'll need your swimsuit and chamois."

Traci tried to hide her disappointment. She didn't want to admit that she was getting a little bored with the floor exercises. Instead, she hurried to change. A few of the younger girls greeted her. They were a little shy.

"My name's Traci," she said. "Since we're classmates, what are your names?"

The girls introduced themselves: Claire, Juana, Tamiqua, Gina. Traci tried to remember the names. She wanted to get along with everyone, even Margo.

The group went through their stretches and calisthenics. Out of the corner of her eye, Traci noticed one of the other girls (Gina? Claire?) staring at her. During the break between stretching and the more demanding exercises, the girl timidly approached Traci.

"Uh, how old are you?" she asked.

"Twelve," Traci replied. "What about you? Is your name Gina?"

The younger girl said, "I'm Claire, and I'm eight. Have you done diving before?"

"No, I've never dived off a board," Traci admitted. "I'm a little nervous about it."

"Oh, it's really cool," Claire exclaimed. "And I think it's great, what you're doing."

"What's great about it?" asked Traci.

"That you're only now just starting in diving, even

44

though you're so old," Claire replied, giving Traci a look of admiration.

"Well, you're never too old to learn new things," Traci said, keeping a straight face.

After the calisthenics, which Traci found a little less exhausting, the girls split into smaller groups. Sophia had Traci demonstrate her approach and hurdle moves.

"Pretty good," Sophia said. "But —"

"But you must be able to do it without looking at the floor." Traci recognized the sharper voice. It was Margo, who had come in without Traci noticing.

"When you dive off a board, you cannot look at your feet. Practice with your head up."

"Okay," Traci said. "I'll work on that."

"Also," said Margo, "you are doing your approach too slowly. The steps must be about this fast." The coach clapped her hands four times. "If your approach is too slow, your dive will be ruined. Also, be careful not to walk too fast, either. Just about like this," she said, clapping her hands again.

Traci nodded, feeling more tense than she had since the last time she had done something with Margo looking on. She wished Sophia had stayed with them, but the assistant coach had left to help the other girls.

"Do the approach again," Margo said. "Without looking at your feet. Your brain will have a memory of the right length for the steps, without you watching. If not, you must practice more. But first, trust your memory."

Traci got on the "board," closed her eyes for a moment, took a deep breath, and did the approach and hurdle again.

"Your first three steps were two inches too long," Margo said, "and your last step was too short. The tempo was better. But you must swing your arms more. You keep them at your sides too much. Once again."

Traci did it again.

"The last step is still too short," Margo said. "Remember, the last step takes you into the hurdle. It is very important. Your head was too stiff. You need flexibility in your spine."

Traci repeated the approach. Margo had more criticisms. After the tenth or eleventh time, Margo said, "Your last step was an inch too short. Have you practiced at home?"

Traci finally lost it. "*Yes*, I must have done it a thousand times! I get confused, with you standing there and giving me all these tiny corrections! I'm new, and those meaningless criticisms make me more and more nervous."

"They are not 'meaningless,'" Margo snapped. "They are *important* corrections, or I would not give them. Nothing in diving is meaningless or unimportant. If you want to be a successful diver, you must demand more of yourself. If you are not willing to demand more of yourself, you will achieve nothing."

Traci saw that the rest of the class had stopped what they were doing and were listening to what Margo was saying.

"What's more, it is good to be nervous," Margo continued, her voice still sharp. "What is bad is to be too relaxed. I hope you will never stop being nervous. That is what will make you do your best."

Traci looked at Sophia. Sophia looked concerned, but Traci couldn't tell whether Sophia felt that Margo was being too tough or just tough enough.

"Sorry," Traci mumbled. "I'm not used to this and I'll keep working, I promise."

Margo gave one of her stiff nods. "If you do, you

will make progress. Now let me see your approach once more."

Traci kept working on the approach and hurdle, and later demonstrated the diver's jump. Margo was satisfied with the jump right away, and eventually had no further comments to make on the approach, either — except to urge Traci to keep working at home and not to make it either too slow or too fast.

Finally Margo said, "It's time for you to change and use the pool."

Traci changed into her swimsuit as fast as she could. Sophia was waiting for her next to a one-meter diving board. She had a small exercise mat, the kind that folded lengthwise, under her arm. Margo was nowhere in sight.

"Is that mat for me?" Traci asked.

Sophia nodded. "We're going to get you started on backward dives today, and for that, you'll be using this mat."

Traci was surprised. "*Backward* dives? I thought I'd be doing forward dives first. I mean, all that drilling on approaches and hurdles — that's for forward dives, right?"

"Right," Sophia said. "When you do backward

48

dives, you stand at the end of the board with your back to the pool. Obviously, you don't do an approach for a backward dive, since you do it from a standing start."

"Okay," said Traci. "But what's the mat for? And why don't I do forward dives, since I've been working on them all this time?"

"Take it easy," Sophia said. "Backward dives are as important as forward dives, and you need to learn the technique for them, too. We've found that the mat is a good introduction."

She swished the mat in the water. "That ought to do it," she said. "Come on."

"Why did you get it wet?" Traci asked.

"To make it slippery. Now take it easy, this is new to you." Sophia had Traci walk out on the board. Sophia followed with the mat.

Traci was startled at how far down the surface of the pool seemed. One meter was just over three feet and hadn't looked like much of a height — until she was looking down from it. The board was much wider than a balance beam, so Traci wasn't worried about falling. Still, the bottom of the pool was a lot farther away than the mats beneath the beam had been.

Sophia handed Traci the mat. "Put it down so the end of the mat is even with the end of the board. Then lie down on it face up, head at the end."

Traci did as she was told. The wet mat felt chilly. Or maybe she was breaking out in goosebumps for some other reason?

"Okay," Sophia said. "Scoot back till your head is off the mat. Lift your feet a little, but don't bend your legs. Point your toes toward me. Reach both arms over your head and clasp your hands together."

Once Traci was in the right position, Sophia said, "In a moment, I'm going to lift the end of the mat under your legs until you slide off into the water. As you do, don't move your head or arch your body and keep your hands clasped. Ready?"

"Uh-huh," replied Traci, holding her position.

Sophia raised the mat, and before Traci had time to feel nervous, she slid into the pool.

As Traci came to the surface, Sophia called out, "You okay? How'd that feel?"

"Fine. Did I do it right?"

"That was a good start. Let's run through it again."

As Traci went back out on the board and lay down on the mat, Sophia said, "You arched your back that time. Try not do to that. Also, don't move your head and keep those toes pointed. Got that?"

"I think so," said Traci. Sophia lifted the mat again, and Traci slid into the pool. This time, it seemed to her that she held her position better and there was less splash on her entry.

Nevertheless, they repeated it several times, with Sophia making corrections, though more gently than Margo would have.

Sophia then had Traci do the slide again, but this time with her arms held straight to the sides and her head lifted so she could watch her feet. As Sophia lifted the mat, Traci raised her arms overhead and moved her head back to the same position as in the previous slides.

It took Traci several repetitions until she was able to get her head and arms into the right position before she hit the water, but she finally did it to Sophia's satisfaction.

"Now we'll do the tuck position," said Sophia. She had Traci lie back on the mat, bend her knees, and wrap her arms around her bent legs. At the same time, Traci lifted her head and tucked her chin against her chest. When Sophia lifted the mat and

Traci began to slide, she moved out of the tuck, straightening her legs and neck into a line and clasping her hands together overhead.

It took Traci much longer to coordinate getting her body into a straight line from the tuck before she hit the water. But eventually she was able to do it a few times in a row. Traci was relieved to be working with Sophia, whose guidance was more supportive than what she felt she'd gotten from Margo.

"One last thing today," said Sophia. "Let's do a roll-off from a tuck position."

This time Sophia positioned the mat so that it hung over the board by two inches. Traci sat at the end of the mat with her back to the water, clasped her knees to her chest, and tucked her chin in. Then she rocked back and straightened out as she entered the pool.

As Traci surfaced, she heard Margo's cold voice. "Kick your legs up before you enter the water, so you enter in a straight line. Visualize your body going into the water straight up and down. Once again."

Traci sighed. Margo was back and so was the harsh attitude. Under Margo's critical eye, she repeated the roll-off over and over, until Margo ran out of faults to find. As Traci climbed out of the pool, tired and chilled, Margo gave the stiff nod that was as close as she ever came to praise. She told Traci she'd see her next session and walked away.

"You did well, Trace," Sophia said.

"I'm glad *someone* thinks so," muttered Traci as she dried herself with her chamois.

"Margo thinks so, too," Sophia insisted. "You'll learn to appreciate her style someday."

Traci doubted that, but didn't contradict Sophia. She just wanted to change into dry clothes and get out of there.

As she was leaving the building, Traci ran into a group of girls her own age carrying gym bags.

"Hi," she said as the girls reached her. "Do you work with Margo?"

"We're her intermediate diving class," said one of them. "What about you?"

Traci introduced herself and explained how she'd come late to diving.

"You're a gymnast?" asked the girl who had spoken first. "You do that balance beam stuff? That's really awesome!"

Traci laughed. "That's funny, I think diving off those high platforms is awesome!"

The group laughed, too, and another girl said, "We're going to this ice cream shop where we hang out sometimes. Want to come?"

"Sure!" said Traci, happy to have found girls her own age to spend time with.

"How are you doing with diving?" asked the first girl.

"I haven't actually dived yet," Traci said, "unless you count sliding off a mat as diving. But someday soon, I hope. I've been working mostly with Sophia."

"Sophia's really neat!" said the girl.

"I like her a lot," Traci agreed. "But I guess I'd like anyone after spending some time with Margo. *She's* really hard to take."

The other girls stared at Traci, who suddenly realized that she might have made a mistake. These girls didn't seem to share her opinion of the coach.

"There's nothing wrong with Margo," said the second girl. "She's a great coach. I wouldn't work with anyone else."

"Me neither," said the first girl. The rest of the group nodded, and their looks at Traci were not friendly anymore.

"Since you haven't even dived yet," the first girl

went on, "you don't know enough to say something like that about Margo."

"Well, I guess not," Traci admitted. "I was only —"

"Until you've been around a little, you should stop bad-mouthing Margo and learn to be a diver."

"Right," said another girl. "Maybe then you'll have a clue what you're talking about."

The group walked away, and Traci knew that she was no longer welcome to go with them. She watched them go, feeling embarrassed and wishing she'd kept her mouth shut. She also began to wonder. All these girls were willing to defend Margo and didn't want to hear anything bad said of her. Apparently there was more to Margo than Traci realized.

7

After dinner, Traci was still feeling upset. She decided to call Valerie and get some much-needed sympathy. When Valerie answered, Traci ran through what had happened that day and then waited for Valerie to offer comfort and support.

Valerie seemed excited that Traci had called. "I've got something to tell you," she said. "But first, tell me how things have been going with you."

Traci spelled it all out for Valerie, then waited for her friend's sympathy. She didn't get what she had hoped for. Instead, Valerie said, "It sounds to me like you spoke out of turn. I mean, how long have you been in these classes? Three sessions? Four?"

"I know I'm not an expert diver," Traci admitted,

"but that doesn't mean I was wrong about Margo. She's not —"

"Trace, you have to earn the right to an opinion," Valerie interrupted. "Until you've earned that right, you'd better be careful what you say, or you're not going to make any friends. Sounds to me like those other girls think Margo's great. Instead of complaining about her, you should think about whether you're right or wrong in your attitude. If Margo's just a bully, how come she gets such great athletes to work with her?"

"I didn't say she was *just* a bully," Traci said, feeling that Valerie wasn't being fair. "All I said was that she —"

"You don't get it," Valerie cut in. "What I'm telling you is that you shouldn't have said *anything*. You're a newcomer. Don't make waves yet. And I still say you're really lucky to be working with someone like Margo. Learn to live with it. That's my advice."

Traci felt like she'd been ambushed. "I *have* been living with it! I've done everything Margo told me to do. I've been doing my homework. I haven't given her any grief. . . . Well, maybe a little."

There was a moment of awkward silence. Then Traci remembered that Valerie had something she wanted to tell her.

"So, what's your news?"

All the excitement returned to Valerie's voice. "I'm changing coaches! This new guy sounds perfect. He worked with the U.S. Olympic team a few years ago, and he wants me for a student! I gave Jeff the bad news today."

"That's great," Traci said, their disagreement forgotten for the moment. "When do you start?"

"In a few days. I'll let you know how it goes, but I'm really pumped! And Trace?"

"Yeah?"

"When I do start, I'm going to keep a really low profile at first. I mean, until I get a sense of how things work there, I won't say anything bad about anyone — especially the guy in charge. It's just common sense."

"Yeah, well," Traci muttered, her sense of betrayal returning. "You're better than me at getting along. Well, see you, and good luck."

Valerie seemed to realize that Traci wasn't happy that she hadn't simply gone along with her complaints. "Trace, don't be angry at me. I know that after working with Jeff, Margo is hard to take. But just take it easy with the bad-mouthing, all right? Or you'll only have more hassles than you already do."

They hung up a few moments later. Deep inside, Traci knew Valerie was right. Valerie was unusually realistic about the world of high-level competitive athletics, and her slant on things was good to get. Traci vowed she'd take her friend's advice.

During her next session with Sophia, Traci continued to do floor and trampoline work with the younger girls. She also spent more time using the mat and working on backward dive entries. She realized that she was improving in several ways. For one thing, her forward dive approach became almost automatic. She could do it without looking at her feet, and at the right speed, and her steps were the right length. Margo had almost no corrections to make, except for the way she swung her arms — she didn't swing them enough — and the way she held her head — she tended to hold it too high.

Traci continued to struggle a little bit with the tuck position on the mat. She found it difficult to coordinate her movement so that she extended her body into a straight line, with her arms fully stretched out, just before her hands hit the water. It was especially hard, she found, when she worked from a sitting position. Sophia was very patient, and Margo was very demanding. It was frustrating, but Traci held her temper and kept working at it.

She ran into the older girls afterward, and they nodded to her. Traci decided to stay away from them for now. Eventually, she wanted to make her peace with them and have friends her own age among the divers. The eight- and nine-year-olds were nice enough, but she didn't have much in common with them.

During the next session, Margo watched Traci do her floor work and her backward "dives" from the mat on the diving board, all without saying a word. Sophia had almost nothing to say, either. As Traci was putting the mat aside, she saw the two coaches talking. At one point, Margo looked over at Traci, who quickly looked away. Traci didn't want Margo to think that she was spying on her.

Finally, Margo called to Traci.

"Today, you will do forward dives from a one-meter board," Margo said. Sophia gave Traci a thumbs-up signal.

Traci discovered that her heart was racing. She'd been eagerly awaiting this chance, and now she was nervous. What if she was awful? Would Margo give her a chance to work through her jitters? Would she be patient? Traci didn't want to admit to being nervous. She simply nodded and said, "Okay."

"We'll keep it simple today," Sophia said. "You'll try forward dives from tuck, pike, and straight positions, and maybe we'll get to some backward dives, too. You ready for this?"

Traci's throat felt dry. She swallowed and said, "I think so, yeah."

Margo nodded and said, "Sophia will work with you now. I'll be back later to look."

Margo left the pool area. Sophia turned to Traci. "Let's begin with the forward dive from the tuck position. You've got the approach and hurdle down, but now you'll do it on a springboard — and that feels very different. When you come down with both feet on the board from the hurdle, the board will flex under your weight and spring up, giving you some lift. That will take getting used to."

As they walked to the board, Sophia continued, "For the tuck, you have to time it so that you pull your thighs into your chest and grab your shins just before you're at the peak of the dive. Then you open up so that your arms stretch your body into a straight line just before your hands hit the surface. Think about the tucks you did on the trampoline. Clear so far?"

Traci nodded, but suddenly *nothing* seemed clear.

"Unless you have questions, let's see you try one." Sophia gestured to the one-meter board. Traci slowly walked out on it. It was scary out there — the water seemed to be very far beneath her feet. She stood like a statue for what felt like several minutes, but probably was only a few seconds.

"Trace? You all right?" asked Sophia.

Traci nodded, unable to speak or move. She didn't want to admit how scared she suddenly felt. Surely, no halfway decent diver felt frightened on a one-meter board!

Sophia walked closer to Traci and began speaking quietly. "I'm going to let you in on a little secret. A lot of divers are scared when they first get on a board or a platform. Even on a one-meter board.

Some divers never get over being scared — even champion divers. That's the truth. There's nothing to be ashamed of. Really."

Traci didn't feel a lot better. She liked Sophia, but found it hard to believe that the coach was telling her the truth. It seemed more likely to her that Sophia was only trying to give Traci a boost in morale.

"Here's a good way to deal with the fear. It worked for me, anyway. Stand there for a few seconds with your eyes closed and *visualize* your dive. Go through it from beginning to end in your mind, everything you'll do. Then open your eyes, take a couple of slow, deep breaths — and *do it*. Just like that. What's the worst that can happen? Maybe you'll be embarrassed, but it won't kill you."

Traci noticed that a few of her young classmates were watching nearby. She suddenly felt angry with herself. She'd done much harder things as a gymnast — and more dangerous things, too.

She closed her eyes, imagined a slow-motion version of the dive, opened her eyes . . . and went into her approach.

It was awful. She didn't get the lift off the board she had expected, didn't straighten out from the tuck soon enough, and hit the water with her stomach. It stung, and there was a really big splash. As she slowly climbed out of the pool, she heard a few younger girls giggling.

Sophia stopped the giggling and came back to Traci. "The next time you'll do better. I'm adjusting the fulcrum of the board to give you more lift. That was part of the problem."

The fulcrum — the point that separated the "springy" part of the board from the fixed part, like the pivot of a seesaw — was adjustable by turning a wheel and sliding a bar forward or back to make the springy section longer or shorter. Sophia shortened it.

"Now you'll get more elevation and have more time to straighten out. Ready?"

"I guess," said Traci. It had to be better this time than the first time. It *had* to. She wouldn't give those little girls anything more to laugh at if she could possibly avoid it.

Sure enough, on her second attempt Traci got higher coming out of the hurdle and was able to straighten out her body, but she was a little too quick. Her legs went past the vertical and her entry was not perpendicular to the surface. But it was better, and didn't hurt at all.

"Good!" Sophia exclaimed. "This time, try to hold your entry position, and as your hands hit the water, flex your fingers back. And keep your ankles together."

The next several dives were not as horrible as the first one had been, but none of them were all that good, either. Traci kept forgetting one thing or another; either her feet weren't together, or her hands weren't right, or she never hit the tuck because her hands slipped off her shins. It looked like there was no end to the different kinds of mistakes you could make. Traci was sure she had made most of them.

Sophia remained cheerful and positive. When Traci tried a forward dive in the pike position — bending at the waist but keeping her legs straight — she did another belly-whopper. At least there were no giggles this time.

"You have to put more energy into the flex when you bend at the waist so you get more forward momentum," Sophia said. "That way, you're more likely to hit the water vertically, not on your belly. Also, focus your eyes on the far end of the pool until you do the hurdle. When you leave the board after the hurdle, focus on the point where you'll enter the water. And try to touch your toes with your hands — that's the sign of a good pike."

Traci did several repetitions. She got better, though she didn't think she was ever really good. It was discouraging. Sophia continued to say nice things, but Traci suspected that she was only being kind.

Traci then dived in the straight position — without bending. At Sophia's suggestion, Traci leaned forward more when coming out of the hurdle. Sophia also told her to spread her arms to the side as she went up and bring them together overhead as she neared the water.

Here, too, Traci was frustrated again and again. She hit the water too soon, before she was straight up-and-down, or too late, splashing hard with the backs of her legs. She lost her balance a couple of times and didn't hit the board with both feet after the hurdle. Once, she leaned too far forward coming off the board and just avoided hitting the water stomach-first.

Her first experience of diving left Traci feeling

very discouraged. Maybe this wasn't her sport, after all. Maybe Margo had been wrong.

After Traci's last messed-up dive in the straight position, Sophia said that she was going to get Margo. Traci tried not to wince. She imagined Margo kicking her out in disgrace.

Sophia returned with Margo. Before Traci got on the board, Sophia took her aside. "Don't worry, you're doing well," she said. "Just visualize your dives, relax, and do them. Don't expect to be perfect. This is only your first day."

On the board, Traci closed her eyes and visualized the dive: hands around shins at the top of the dive, then straightening smoothly into the water, arms extended.

This time, her tuck was tight. She straightened out . . . and hit the water before she had straightened all the way. *Splat.* Not good.

When she went for the pike position, she knew before she hit the water that she had come out of the pike too soon, and that her back was arched too much. But she didn't make a huge splash. Better — a little.

The straight dive was pretty bad, Traci thought. In

her nervousness, she forgot to stretch her arms to the side before reaching over her head. Also, she didn't lean forward enough, so her entry was short of the ideal straight up-and-down. Sighing, Traci climbed out of the pool and dried herself with her chamois, waiting for Margo to jump all over her.

But, surprisingly, Margo didn't say much. She simply pointed out that Traci had a lot of work to do. She made no specific criticisms at all and told Traci she'd see her at the next session.

Traci was relieved to have been spared a harsh scolding, but she still felt depressed as she changed. She walked by the older girls and barely noticed them, lost in a cloud of gloom.

As she plodded home, Traci found it impossible to imagine that she could ever be a decent diver, let alone a great one.

8

Since Traci had the next day off from diving, she agreed to go shopping with Valerie. Traci biked to Valerie's house and they rode to the mall together. When they sat down at a snack shop in the food court, Valerie's excitement was clear.

"I met my new coach and he's *awesome!* What a difference from Jeff! This guy pumps you up when he just talks to you! He thinks I've got major potential, but says I'd better be ready for the hardest work I've ever done. And I'm like, 'Sure! That's what I want!' And he smiles and goes, 'I think you'll do fine.' I can't believe it, it's too good to be true."

Traci felt happy for her friend and tried to show it, but her spirits were so low that Valerie couldn't help noticing.

"You don't look so great," she said. "That coach still giving you a hard time?"

Traci shook her head. "It isn't Margo. I don't know. This may be a mistake."

"*What* may be a mistake?" asked Valerie. "Working with Margo? I still think she's —"

"I told you, it isn't Margo. It's *me*. I got my first chance to dive yesterday. Really dive, off a springboard. And I was *awful*."

Valerie stared at her friend. "Trace, it was your *first day*. Hello? What did you think, that you'd ace it like a gold-medal winner the first time? I don't believe you were awful. I think you were inexperienced. And it showed."

Traci waved off Valerie's explanation. "It wasn't just that I didn't dive well. When I got on that board, I was *scared*. I could barely get myself to move at all!"

"But you did dive, right?" Valerie asked.

"Yeah, I did — after Sophia, the assistant coach, gave me a pep talk. And I was the pits! I don't have any talent for diving. If I can't dive, and I can't be a gymnast, I don't know. I better forget about being an athlete altogether."

"Whoa!" Valerie said, holding up her hands. "That sounds pretty extreme. Look, you had a bad day, and now you're overreacting, that's all."

Traci laughed, but without humor. "I had a 'bad day'? After all my years on the balance beam, it turns out I'm afraid of heights! On a *one-meter board!* What'll I do on a three-meter board? Or a ten-meter platform? That's not a 'bad day,' Val. That's a total disaster!"

When Valerie started to laugh, Traci couldn't believe it.

"I'm sorry, Trace," Valerie said, still chuckling. "I'm just remembering when we started out in gymnastics class. We were terrified! Vaulting over a horse scared us, getting on a balance beam, even one that was barely above the floor, scared us! I started to cry, and you stood like a statue. Remember?"

Traci couldn't help smiling. "Yeah, we were pretty pathetic. But we were *little kids.* Four years old! Sure, we were scared. I'm twelve now, and I shouldn't feel that way."

Valerie shrugged. "Why not? You're doing something new. Did you say anything to Margo or Sophia about being scared?"

"Well, Sophia told me that most divers are that way at first," Traci admitted. "But Sophia's nice, and I think she only wanted to make me feel better."

"Well, I think you just have to stick with it for a while and you'll get past this. I know you, and I'm sure you can do whatever it takes." She finished her soda and grabbed her bag.

"Oh, I almost forgot," she said. "I know a girl who's a student of Margo's, a girl in my class named Carly Freed. She said she'd be happy to talk to you if you like. Want to call her when we get home?"

Traci agreed. When they got through to Carly, they made arrangements to eat lunch together at school the next day.

Traci's mind wandered throughout classes the next morning. What would Carly have to say about Margo?

At lunchtime, Traci and Valerie grabbed a table. Valerie scanned the room, then pointed at a tall girl with dark hair. "That's her. Hey, Carly!" she shouted.

Traci recognized her as the first girl to speak up to defend the coach when Traci had bad-mouthed her. From Carly's expression, it was clear that she recognized Traci, too. But she said nothing about it.

The three girls spread their lunches out and started eating.

"Listen," Traci said as soon as she could, "I want to say that I was out of line the other day. What I said about Margo, that was wrong."

Carly seemed to relax. "Okay. Just about everyone who works with Margo thinks she's pretty great, including me. You'll see for yourself, eventually."

Traci sighed. "If there *is* an 'eventually.' I'm not sure there will be."

"How come? Are you thinking of quitting already?" asked Carly.

Traci shook her head and said, "Maybe I'll get thrown out. Diving may not be my sport."

Carly stared at Traci. "But you just started! How can you tell so soon?"

Traci explained about her fear on a one-meter springboard. "That isn't the kind of thing a good diver has to worry about, right?"

Carly laughed. "*Wrong!* Totally wrong!"

Valerie flashed Traci a grin. "See?"

"I've known maybe a hundred divers," Carly said, "and most of them were frightened when they first started diving. I think it's the way most people are.

The first time I got on a diving board, I couldn't move at all! I wanted to climb back down the ladder and go home."

"How old were you?" Traci asked.

"Eight. But it doesn't matter," Carly said. "There are divers in my group who are *still* scared every time they dive. And they're our age. They manage to deal with it somehow."

Traci felt a little better. "What about you? Are you still scared?"

"Not as much as I once was. But I still get butter-flies. Especially on a platform, for some reason." Carly leaned forward and looked hard at Traci.

"If you think that being scared is enough of a rea-son to quit diving, you're wrong. And if you think that Margo is going to give up on you, you're wrong again. If Margo thinks you can be a diver, she'll stand by you. And if she told you she thinks you can be a good diver, believe it."

"That's what I've been telling her," Valerie said, waving her hands in the air. "Maybe she'll believe it coming from you, since you've been there."

"How did you get used to diving when you were afraid?" Traci asked.

Carly thought for a moment before replying. "The more I dived, the less the fear got to me. It didn't go away, but it changed, somehow. Now the butterflies give me a kind of jolt, a charge of, I don't know, excitement and anticipation. It's like my nerves are tingling and every part of me is focused on the dive. Does that make sense?"

Traci nodded slowly. "You know what? It does. It's the way I used to feel right before starting my routine on the balance beam. I felt electric."

"Exactly!" Carly said, grinning.

Valerie laughed and turned to Carly. "Trace was an awesome gymnast, until she suddenly got so tall and her knees started giving her trouble. She was almost as good as me!"

"*Almost?*" Traci yelled in mock outrage. "You never saw the day you could do a balance beam routine as good as mine!"

"Well, with my new coach, I'll ace the balance beam soon. I bet he's as good as Margo," Valerie answered.

"Margo's something else," Carly said, the admiration in her voice clear. "And, Traci, you'll find out that she really cares about everyone she works with.

I can't really say more than that, because Margo doesn't like us to brag about her. But she'd do anything for us — and we'd do anything for her."

Traci sat back and thought about Carly's devotion to the coach. Margo must have done something to deserve it. Then and there, she told herself that she'd master her fear of the board and her anxiety over Margo somehow. And that she'd keep on with her diving.

During the next month, Traci found that Carly had been right. Her fear was slowly changing into that electric kind of jolt they'd talked about. Traci never relaxed completely on a springboard, but maybe that was a good thing. It was what Margo had said early on: Being nervous meant you paid attention more — and weren't as likely to mess up or get hurt.

At the same time, her diving improved. A week after learning simple forward dives, Traci began working on backward dives. She started with a simple backward dive in the straight position.

"As you jump," Sophia said, "arch your back and neck to see the water as you enter."

On Traci's first try, she didn't keep her body straight and hit the water with a huge splash. But she didn't get upset. She knew that she wasn't expected to be perfect right away. She climbed out of the pool, looked at Sophia, and said, "Oops."

Sophia laughed. "You arched your back, but you didn't keep those muscles tense, so you bent into a sort of tuck. Keep your muscles tight and stay in a straight line this time."

Traci got better until, on her last try, she was almost vertical on her entry. Sophia's grin showed Traci that she had done well.

Traci then went on to the backward dive in a tuck position. "This is tougher," said Sophia. "As you jump, you have to lean away from the board a little to get clear of it when you come down. On the way up, bring your knees to your chest and grab your shins; then straighten and use a 'lateral entry.' That means —"

"I know," Traci cut in, smiling. "I stretch my arms to the side and then overhead in my come-out. Right?"

"You're getting to be an expert," Sophia replied. "Let's see the dive."

Standing with her back to the pool, Traci made

sure that her heels overhung the end of the board. She closed her eyes and visualized the dive: the tuck, the come-out, and the entry. She bent her knees and jumped. The dive was far from perfect — she hit the water before her hands came together — but it wasn't bad. The next attempts were better.

The backward dive in the pike position was less trouble for Traci. "These backward dives are easier for me than the forward ones," she told Sophia. "Is that weird, or normal?"

"Divers often have less trouble with backward dives," Sophia said. "Maybe because you don't have to worry about an approach."

The same day Traci started on backward dives, she added a new skill to her frontward dives: somersaults. As a gymnast, Traci figured that somersaults wouldn't be too hard for her, and she was partly right. She was all right doing a frontward one-and-a-half somersault dive in the tuck position. Traci was supposed to do a complete spin in the air and come down to enter the water headfirst. Sophia had her lean forward as she left the board to get the somersault started. Traci picked it up quickly.

The same dive in the pike position, however —
spinning with her legs straight and bending only
at the waist — was harder. Sophia said, "You need
more forward lean, and try to get higher off the
board."

After a bad dive in which she hit the water before
coming out of the pike, Traci got better.

"Want to try two and a half somersaults?" Sophia
asked.

Traci felt confident. "Why not?" But when she
tried it, she lost sight of the water and hit the surface
flat on her back. The mistake bothered her more
than the pain.

"How do you keep track of where you are when
you're spinning like that?" she asked Sophia.

"It's called 'visual spotting,'" Sophia said. "The
idea is to pick out something that you can see each
time you spin around." She pointed to a clock on the
wall facing the springboard. "Use the clock. Each
time you see it, you've completed another somersault. When you've done your last one, it's time for
your come-out."

Traci looked at the clock. "I'll try." Sure enough,
she found that watching for the clock as she turned

helped keep her from getting lost. But she still didn't have enough time to straighten out before reaching the water.

"You need more lean," Sophia said, "and you need to get more spring from your legs when you leave the board."

On her fifth attempt, Traci bent her knees and sprang upward as hard as she could. She had enough lift to finish her come-out and hit the water with her body in a straight line.

But Traci couldn't do a two-and-a-half somersault dive in the pike position. She couldn't finish the spins in time, even after several attempts.

"It's okay," said Sophia. "You're doing great! Margo has exercises to strengthen your legs and give you extra lift."

Margo came to see Traci's progress at every session. She would always give Traci some pointers for her to work on. Traci started writing them in a notebook and studied it every day. Margo never praised Traci, but Sophia provided plenty of support.

Several sessions later, Traci began working on reverse and inward dives. Though Traci was more self-assured now, she found these dives scary because she had to tumble *toward* the board instead of away from it.

In reverse dives, the diver faces the pool but does *backward* somersaults. For inward dives, the diver's back is to the pool and she does forward somersaults. Either way, Traci worried that she might bang her head against the edge of the board. She said this to Sophia when the coach described the dives.

Sophia said, "Most divers worry about that at first. But when you come off the board, your momentum carries you away from the edge so that you aren't going to collide. Watch."

For the first time, Sophia actually demonstrated dives to Traci. She started with a reverse one-and-a-half somersault in a tuck position. She did an approach and hurdle. As she sprang from the board, she did a tight backward roll, coming out and entering the water with barely any splash. Traci noticed two things: first, that Sophia was a really great diver and second, that Sophia missed the edge of the board by a couple of feet.

"*Awesome!*" Traci whispered. "I didn't know how good you are!"

Sophia smiled as she dried herself off. "See how far I was from the board? Also, I arched my back as I started up, which got me into the somersault. Now I'll do an inward one-and-a-half somersault in the pike position."

Sophia stood at the end of the board with her back to the pool and her heels off the board's edge. Bending her knees deep and swinging her arms up, she jumped high off the board and outward. She bent at the waist and kept her legs straight until her forehead almost touched her shins — a perfect pike — then spun in a forward somersault, toward the board. But, as with the reverse dive, she missed the edge by plenty, straightened into a beautiful come-out, and plummeted into the water smoothly. Traci and the other girls applauded. It was an amazing dive.

Traci began working on inward and reverse dives and soon got over the fear she had felt. It was clear that if she took the time to visualize each dive before she started it she'd stayed out of danger. She was far from perfect, but she sensed that she was making progress.

Traci was now doing four kinds of dives: forward,

backward, inward, and reverse. She had learned the straight, tuck, and pike positions. She was managing pretty well with one-and-a-half somersault dives and improving with two-and-a-half somersaults. Thanks to Margo's leg exercises, which Traci did every day, her legs were getting noticeably stronger and she was able to get more height when she left the board.

"You're not ready for three-and-a-half somersaults," Sophia said, "but you will be before too long. I'd like you to start working on twists. But before you do, I want to see you do some work on the trampoline. Put on your sweats and meet me in the exercise room."

A somersault involves "rolling" forward (or backward), while a twist is like a dancer's pirouette or a figure skater's spin on an ice rink. The most difficult dives combine somersaults *and* twists. These dives score the most points when divers do them well, but they are also the ones that are most likely to be done badly.

Traci wasn't worried about twists. She was comfortable with them from gymnastics. Some of her balance beam dismounts and some of her vaults had included twists. She knew how to get a twist started by turning her upper body to the left or right while she was in the air.

As Traci warmed up on the trampoline in the exercise room, Sophia came in with Margo. Traci felt a tingle of nervousness, which always happened when she knew Margo was watching her.

Margo didn't say anything as Traci went through some maneuvers on the trampoline that included twists and somersaults. She did single and double somersaults with twists. At Sophia's request, she then did somersaults with one and a half and two full twists. Although Traci hadn't done this kind of thing in some time, she felt at ease doing it — or she would have, if Margo hadn't been following every move with that sharp, critical expression on her face.

When Traci had finished, Sophia said, "Give us a minute, Trace."

She and Margo moved away and talked for a minute. Then they approached Traci.

Margo said, "Traci, you are finished with this group."

Traci stared at the coach. Was it possible that Margo was kicking her out?

"Starting next time," Margo went on, "you will be working with me and the more advanced girls."

Sophia beamed at Traci, who felt like she had just won a gold medal.

10

Traci couldn't wait to tell Valerie about her promotion. Since Valerie had started with her new coach, the two friends hadn't seen much of each other outside of school. But Valerie was in when Traci called that evening, and she invited Traci over after dinner.

As soon as the girls were in Valerie's room, Traci burst out with her good news. Valerie smiled, but the smile was weak.

"Hey, great, Trace. Congratulations. I'm really happy for you."

Traci said, "I'll see Carly more now. Of course, I'll also see more of Margo — in fact I'll see her all the time, because Sophia mostly works with the younger divers, but actually, I can handle Margo. The main thing is, I've been making good progress."

"Definitely," Valerie said, and looked out the window.

Traci looked closely at her friend. "Val, what's going on? Are you okay?"

Valerie sighed and flopped back on her bed. "I'm all right. I mean, I'm not sick or anything. But I'm not doing so great lately."

"Why?" Traci asked. "Don't tell me it's your new coach! I thought he was supposed to be fantastic! You mean he isn't?"

"Oh, he's okay, but I'm not sure how good *I* am," Valerie said. "The other people in this class are unbelievably good, and I don't know if I can cut it. I'm not as great as I used to think I was."

Traci shook her head. "I don't believe it! You're a fantastic athlete! You were the best one in our class by a mile!"

Valerie stared up at the ceiling. "Yeah, right . . . *our* class. But that was just a bunch of kids. I see that now. In this group, I'm at the bottom. They do things I don't believe I can ever do. It's been . . . I don't know *what* it's been. I figured I'd always be in control, that nothing would ever get me down. Well, guess what? I was wrong."

"Wait a second!" Traci stood up and looked down at her friend. She'd never seen Valerie look depressed or beaten until now. "Remember a few weeks ago? I said that I was going to quit, and you told me to hang in there, that I wasn't giving myself a fair chance? Does that sound familiar? Because here we go again, except now, you're playing my part."

Valerie shook her head. "This is different. You were starting in a brand-new sport. I'm doing what I've been doing all my life! I'm just finding out I've been clueless all this time! Now that I compare myself to first-class athletes, I see I'm nothing special."

"I don't believe it!" Traci insisted. "You say my case was different. It was in some ways, but in other ways, no. The fact is that you made a big jump, too, just like I did.

"I know, diving is a different sport, but still, when you move into new level of talent, it's going to be a shock. You were used to being numero uno. In Jeff's class, everyone looked up to you. Jeff kept going on about how you were the greatest ever, and we all naturally felt the same way. *I* sure did! Now, all of a sudden, you're not the best."

Valerie turned her head away, but Traci didn't stop.

"I'm going to say what you said to me a few weeks back — and I know it's true. You're selling yourself short, and you're letting the sudden change get to you too much. And you're giving in way too easy."

Valerie only sighed. "If you saw these guys, you'd know. They're out of my league."

"You think they started that way?" Traci asked. "You think they were all-stars when they were in diapers? I bet when they started in this class, they went through what you're going through now. And they shook it off and got back to work and got better."

She sat down next to her friend and spoke more gently. "That's what you'll do, too. You'll get up off the ground and suck it up and get to work. You're a fighter, and you're an athlete. You've got talent and drive. And I do *not* believe that you're going to just walk away from the thing you've been working toward all your life. I bet that in a few weeks, you'll remember today and say, 'What was I thinking?' You'll *laugh*. You've hit a little bump in the road, that's all. You didn't hit a wall."

Finally, Valerie sat up. She looked at Traci with a small smile. "Listen to you!" she said. "I'll tell you one thing: Being in that class has sure changed your attitude. You're a lot tougher than you used to be."

Traci was pleased. "You think so? Well, good, then. And I think the same thing will happen to you. You have what it takes. Wait and see, you'll get past this. When this coach said that you could go to the top, he knew what he was talking about. Just hang in there."

Valerie laughed. "All right, all right, I'll hang in there, just to keep you quiet. Thanks."

"That's what friends are for," Traci replied, satisfied.

11

Traci decided that working with a more advanced group of divers had its good and bad points. On the plus side, she was with girls her own age, including Carly. Once the other girls saw that Carly had forgiven Traci, they were friendly. She often went out with some of them for a snack after workouts. Also, Traci found she liked working with divers who challenged her to improve. When she was challenged in this way, she *did* improve.

On the minus side, it could be discouraging to see how much better some of these divers were. A few could do dives that were far beyond anything Traci could manage, at least at this time. A three-and-a-half somersault inward dive in the pike position with a twist, for example, was a dive Traci could only dream about performing.

Even though Traci no longer thought that having Margo watching her all the time was a bad thing, exactly, it did make her uncomfortable. She mentioned it to Carly one day after a workout, when they were with a group of girls. Most of them laughed.

"Sure you're uncomfortable," Carly said. "That doesn't make you different. We *all* are. But, when you think about it, it's a good way to feel. It keeps us on our toes so we don't get too casual and mess up dives because our brains are elsewhere. That's one reason why Margo is such a good coach: She will never let you get too relaxed."

"Is relaxation so terrible?" Traci asked.

Another diver named Rachel said, "Relaxation is okay, but being *too* relaxed isn't, if you want to do your best."

"What are other reasons Margo is so good?" Traci wanted to know.

"For one thing," said Carly, "she doesn't miss a thing. She spots the tiniest flaw in a dive. You probably understand by now that even little mistakes mess up dives. It's not like some other sports, where you can adjust in the middle and things may come out right. In diving, when you make a mistake, you're out of luck. If it happens in competition, well, you're done. Margo never lets a mistake go by. She has a great eye."

"Anything else?" asked Traci.

"She really cares about us," said Rachel "We know she'll be there for us, whatever happens."

Traci wanted to hear more about this, but the others wouldn't go into details. Carly spoke for them all when she said, "You'll find out one day. Margo doesn't like us to talk about these things."

After Traci had been with the advanced group for a week, Margo told her, "Today you'll start on a three-meter board."

Traci had been thinking about this and dreading it. *Three meters!* That was almost ten feet! She was afraid that she might get up there and freeze in panic. She would humiliate herself in front of these girls and never be able to look them in the face again. She thought about talking to Sophia about her fear. But she didn't see much of the other coach now.

She noticed that Carly was standing by herself and went over to her. "I'm supposed to use a three-meter board today."

"Great!" Carly said. "You'll be fine."

Traci leaned forward to whisper so nobody else would overhear her. "You don't get it. I'm scared about that height. What if I can't do it?"

Carly said, "Whatever you did on the one-meter board, you just do the same thing. Visualize the dive. Focus. Concentrate. Don't let yourself think about *anything* except the dive, the things you have to do."

When Traci didn't seem convinced, Carly sighed. "There's no magic trick, no secret. Either you can do it . . . or you can't. Just go up and do the *same* approach, the *same* hurdle. . . . Okay? You're a good athlete and a good diver, and I'm sure you'll do great. But saying that is the only help I can give you."

Traci saw that Carly was right. She remembered the first time she'd been on a diving board and what Sophia had said. Carly was basically telling her the same thing. She managed to smile at Carly.

"I'll be all right. Thanks."

Margo told Traci that her first dive from three meters should be a forward one-and-a-half somersault in the tuck position. "Remember," Margo added, "you don't have to worry about getting a strong jump for height, because you have enough height to begin with. Any questions?"

Traci shook her head and climbed slowly to the higher board. As she reached the top, she looked down. The water seemed to be a long way away. Margo and Carly were watching her, and they were too far away to be of any help. She was on her own.

Traci did what she always did on the lower board. She closed her eyes and visualized the dive, took a deep breath, and started her approach.

She was surprised to find that habit took over. She did her hurdle and jumped, leaning forward to start her somersault. She went into her tuck, bringing her legs up to her chest and grabbing her shins, and straightened out as she plummeted toward the water.

It seemed to take forever to get there, and by the time she did, Traci had gone past the vertical line she had wanted for her entry. Her legs flopped forward too far and the backs of her legs splashed way too much. But she had *done the dive*. She was in the water!

Traci surfaced and swam to the edge of the pool. As she climbed out, Carly gave her a thumbs-up signal. Traci knew that it wasn't for the dive itself, which had been pretty bad. It was for having done it at all.

"Once again," Margo said, "and remember to adjust for the greater height of the board. You should take more time in your come-out and be sure to keep your body tense as you prepare for your entry. Make certain your arms are fully extended."

Traci nodded as she dried herself with the chamois. Then she started up the ladder again. Margo's criticisms were completely right, of course. And Traci knew that, this time, she would do better. More important, she knew that she could master her fear.

For the next few sessions, Traci worked from the three-meter board. She tried to remember that she had more time for somersaults. She worked on all the dives she had learned on the one-meter board: backward, reverse, and inward dives, as well as forward ones; dives in the tuck, pike, and straight positions. Margo's steady stream of comments and corrections gave Traci so much to think about that she almost forgot to worry about the three-meter height.

During her second week using a three-meter board, Traci did her first successful three-and-a-half somersault dives, both tuck and pike. She barely had time to feel proud of her accomplishment before Margo had her begin working on adding one and even two twists to these dives.

As she came up from the pool after performing a three-and-a-half somersault dive with two twists in the pike position, she was surprised to see Sophia waiting for her. Traci hadn't seen Sophia by the pool in several weeks.

"I can't believe how far you've gotten since I saw you dive," Sophia said. "You almost nailed that dive, and it's got a pretty high degree of difficulty."

Traci had learned how judges score dives in competition. A judge awards a dive a point total from 0 to 10. Ten means that the dive is perfect. A score like 8.8 means that the dive is very good. Scores such as 5.5 or less indicate that the dive is pretty poor.

The point totals are then multiplied by a figure called the "degree of difficulty." Every kind of dive has a degree of difficulty rating assigned by an international committee that regulates diving competitions. A relatively easy one, like a simple forward dive in a tuck position, is rated at 1.4. A very hard dive — such as a backward three-and-a-half somersault dive in a tuck position — gets 3.4.

This means that a perfect performance of a very easy dive doesn't score as well as a very good — but *not* perfect — performance of a hard dive. If you don't attempt difficult dives in competition, you might perform well, but you won't win.

Pleased by Sophia's praise, Traci said, "I still have a long way to go, but thanks."

"Sure you do. But Margo was right about you," replied Sophia.

Before Traci could ask what Margo had said, Margo herself joined them. "Sophia is here to help me with a simulated competition," Margo said.

"What's that?" asked Traci.

Margo explained. "Some of you will do five dives each, the same five. Sophia and I will act as judges and score the dives for quality, just as judges do in real competitions."

The rest of the girls gathered around. "There will be no winners or losers," Margo continued. "I want to give some of you who have not competed a chance to experience how these events work. Each diver will get the list of dives. The standard rules of competition will apply. Divers have to complete each dive within a time limit. They must keep their lists handy and do the dives in the right order. Once a diver is on the board, if she does not do the correct dive, or fails to dive, her score will be zero."

"I understand," Traci said.

"Good, because I want you to be one of the divers," Margo said. "None of the dives you will do is beyond your present level of skill. And, as I said, there will be no winners or losers. But you will have an idea of how competitions are run. Also, this is being videotaped." Margo pointed to a woman holding a camcorder. "You'll get cassettes of your dives to study."

Traci nodded, her mouth suddenly dry. She was certain that all the other girls in this group were still much better than she was, no matter how much she had improved lately.

Four girls were in the group in addition to Traci. When Traci read the list of dives that they were to do, she was relieved to see that she had done all of them. The most difficult was a two-and-a-half somersault reverse dive in a tuck position.

The girls drew numbers from a box to determine the order in which they'd dive. Traci was to be the fourth one in each round. The first dive on the list was a backward one-and-a-half somersault in the pike position.

The first diver did what looked to Traci to be a pretty good dive. The pike was not perfect. The girl didn't bend enough, but her entry was fine. Margo gave the girl a 6.5 and Sophia rated it a 7. The second diver had a problem with her approach and messed up her entry badly. Both coaches awarded only 4.5. The third diver, whom Tracy barely knew to say hello to, *aced* it. It was a beautiful pike, a well-timed come-out, and a straight up-and-down entry. She received scores of 9.2 from Margo and 9.4 from Sophia.

Traci went out on the board and paused, closing her eyes as she always did to visualize her actions. Her approach and hurdle were smooth, and she got good lean into the dive. But she didn't quite finish her come-out, and her entry was rushed. She got the same score from both coaches: 6.5. The last diver also got a 6.5.

On the next two dives, Traci did somewhat better. Her third, a one-and-a-half inward somersault in a tuck position, earned her a 7 from Margo and a 7.2 from Sophia — the second-highest score among the five divers.

On the fourth dive, a forward two-and-a-half somersault in a tuck, Traci lost concentration. She mistimed her entry and landed on her back with a loud *splat*. It got her a 3.5 — the lowest score any of the girls had gotten.

Traci felt angry at herself, and the anger helped her to focus hard on the last of the dives: a one-and-a-half reverse somersault with a twist in a pike position. Her approach was fine, and she got good elevation off the board. Traci knew that her pike was good — her forehead touched her legs, and she thought her entry was outstanding.

She scored two 8.5s — her best marks. Traci felt that she had done well enough. At least she knew she had not embarrassed herself.

Margo nodded to Traci at the end of the session, meaning that she was satisfied. "You'll get the cassette tomorrow," she said. "Study it carefully. In ten days, there is going to be an exhibition, with real judges. You'll be one of the divers. I think you're ready."

Traci hoped that Margo was right.

12

The next few sessions were busy ones for Traci. She learned a couple of new dives and worked hard to polish the ones she already knew. She learned that for the exhibition she would choose her own dives. There would be five in all, and she would have to decide for herself how difficult her choices would be.

Valerie called her one evening to ask if Traci wanted to split a pizza for dinner. After asking her mother, Traci agreed to meet Valerie a little later.

While they waited for their order, Traci studied Valerie for clues to how her friend was feeling. Finally, she said, "You look better than the last time I saw you."

Valerie put down her drink and smiled. "I *am* better. I mean, gymnastics is better. I'm still not numero uno or anything, but I'm really working again, and the coach is happy."

Traci smiled. "So you're not planning to quit just yet, huh?"

"No way," Valerie said as the waiter put their pepperoni and mushroom pizza on the table. "And you were a big help."

Traci shrugged and reached for a slice. "It was no big deal."

Valerie replied. "It *was* a big deal, as far as I'm concerned. I'd never lost confidence before, not even for a second. I thought that was *it*, I was toast. You made me see that I was totally wrong. Thank you."

"You're welcome." Traci wiped some cheese off her hand with a napkin. "You can call us even. You did the same thing for me."

"We're the same kind of person as far as sports goes," said Valerie. "We both want to take it to the limit, go the distance. We each know how the other one's mind works. That's why we helped each other through these situations. It takes someone who knows what's happening."

Traci thought as she chewed on a bite of pizza. "I

guess that's right. I've learned something about myself since I started working with Margo. I found out that I really do want to see what I've got. I'm willing to push myself, and I work harder when someone else pushes me. I was worried that I'd be afraid to dive off a three-meter board, but you know what? I've learned how to concentrate until my fear sort of fades away. It doesn't disappear, but it shrinks, and then I can handle it."

Valerie nodded. "And *I've* learned that when I find myself facing tougher competition than I was used to, it revs me up. When the bar is raised, I'll do whatever it takes to get over it."

Traci frowned. "What happens if we don't make it to the top?"

"I don't know," admitted Valerie. "I guess I'll be disappointed. But as long as I know that I gave it all I could, I won't be destroyed, you know what I mean?"

"Yeah," Traci said. "I do. The same thing goes for me, I think."

A few days later, Traci was working on a dive that she was considering for the exhibition: a two-and-a-half somersault inward dive in a pike position. She thought that if she could nail this one it would be a big help in her final score. On the other hand, if she messed it up, it could be a disaster. She decided she'd have to try several more until she was confident she could do it well. If not, then she'd use the —

"Traci?"

Startled, Traci turned to find her mother standing there, looking very upset.

"Mom? What's the matter?" Traci knew just from Mrs. Winchell's expression that something was very wrong.

Traci's mother took a deep breath to calm herself before speaking. "It's your brother. Pete's been in an accident."

Traci stared at Mrs. Winchell. "Is he all right? What happened?"

"His bike was hit by a car. He's been taken to the emergency room at County Medical. Your dad is there with him, and we'll meet him there."

Traci rushed to her mother and the two hugged, forgetting completely that Traci was wearing a wet swimsuit. "How is he doing? What did you hear?"

Mrs. Winchell stood back and shook her head.

"He's unconscious, and they're still running tests. That's all we know for now, honey. Get dried off, and I'll wait for you here."

Traci noticed Margo heading their way with a questioning look on her face. Quickly she explained what had happened to Pete. "I have to go to the hospital with my mother."

"Of course you must," Margo said, looking worried. "I'll wait here with your mother while you get dressed."

Traci hurried into the locker room and changed into street clothes. It seemed to take forever, but she finished as quickly as she could and ran to join her mother. There was little talk between them as they drove to the hospital.

"Pete *was* wearing his helmet, wasn't he?" Traci asked.

"He always wears it," said Mrs. Winchell. "I'm sure he was."

When they walked quickly into the ER waiting room, Mr. Winchell stood up and hugged Traci. He looked pale and shaken. Before Traci could ask, he spoke.

"He's still unconscious. The doctor says that there

may be nerve damage, but it's impossible say how severe it is, or even if there is any at all. And there's still no way of knowing how full a recovery he'll make. But there's a very good chance he'll be fine. They did some kind of reflex test and the results were encouraging, they say."

The three Winchells sat down to wait. Around them, other people came and went. Babies howled, people walked or limped in and walked out with bandaged arms. Across the room, Traci saw a young couple talking quietly to each other, looking as if they, too, were waiting for news about a loved one. A television set was on in the corner of the waiting room, but nobody seemed to be watching it.

Traci picked up a magazine and put it down again without opening it. A doctor in a blue surgical gown came through a door, went over to the young couple, and spoke to them. The young woman gasped, and the young man hugged her tightly. Had they gotten bad news? There was no way to tell. The doctor left and the couple sat down again.

"I think he'll be fine," said Mr. Winchell after what seemed like an endless silence. "Pete's tough. He'll come through."

"Sure he will, Daddy," Traci said, more out of a need to say something positive than because she believed it.

Traci looked at the clock on the wall and realized that they had been waiting for an hour. It seemed like much more time had passed.

The door to the waiting room was under the clock. It opened just as Traci was checking the time. To her amazement, Traci saw Margo come into the room. Margo headed straight for her.

"How is your brother? Have you had any news?"

"Uh . . . no, nothing. The last we heard, he was still unconscious, and they don't know anything yet for sure," Traci stammered. She hadn't recovered from the surprise of seeing the coach.

Margo greeted Traci's mother, who introduced the coach to Mr. Winchell. Sitting down between Traci and Mrs. Winchell, she asked, "Can I be of help in any way? Is there anyone I could call? Would you like anything to eat or drink? I can go to the cafeteria while you wait here."

Nobody wanted anything, so Margo stayed put. Mr. Winchell leaned across his wife and said, "Margo, we're very grateful to you for coming by, but there's no need for you to stay. We can manage here."

Margo smiled. "I'll sit for a little while, if you don't mind."

"Of course we don't," said Traci's mother. "And thank you."

Margo turned and said, "Your daughter is a gifted athlete. It's been a pleasure having her in my classes. I only wish I could have told you under happier circumstances."

Margo talked about Traci's progress for a little while and then said, "I remember when my younger sister had an accident, years ago. She was a little daredevil and she fell out of a tree. She, too, was unconscious for quite some time. But she recovered fully — as I'm sure Pete will, too. I remember how worried my family was, and how upset I was. I blamed myself for not having kept a closer watch on her. But it all turned out well."

Margo's quiet, pleasant conversation helped to keep the Winchell family's mind off the subject of Pete, whose condition they still did not know. Another half hour went by, and a different doctor appeared in the waiting room. He saw the Winchells and walked over. He looked very tired.

"How is Pete?" asked Traci. "Is he awake?"

"He regained consciousness a few minutes ago," the doctor said. "I'm not absolutely certain yet, but all the signs are encouraging. We'd like to keep him here for another day for a few tests and to keep him under observation, but it doesn't seem that he suffered any permanent nerve damage."

Mr. Winchell put his arm around his wife, who asked, "Can we see him?"

"For a few minutes," said the doctor. "He's tired and needs his sleep. You can certainly spend more time with him tomorrow, and the next day, barring complications, he can go home."

Margo stood up and put on her coat, preparing to leave. Traci put a hand on the coach's arm.

"Thank you. It was really great of you to come and stay with us."

Margo smiled. "It was the least I could do. Don't forget, you're one of my girls, now." Margo turned to Traci's parents. "I'm delighted that your son is doing well. And now I'd better be leaving. Traci, don't come in tomorrow if you don't feel up to it."

"Thanks, coach," Traci said. "I guess I'll see how it goes."

Mrs. Winchell held Margo's hand for a moment. "We're very grateful, not only for you coming tonight, but for your work with Traci."

"Thank you," said Mr. Winchell, "and good night."

As Margo left the waiting room, Traci watched her go. She remembered Carly saying that there was more to the coach than Traci could see.

Now Traci was beginning to understand what Carly had meant.

13

The next afternoon, Traci went to visit Pete in the hospital. He had been moved to a regular room and, aside from some scrapes and bruises, was in pretty good shape.

"They're sending me home tomorrow," he said. "I think I'll be able to see your diving exhibition. I'll sure try, anyway."

"Great!" Traci said. "Did you hear about Margo?"

"Your coach? What about her?"

Traci sat on the edge of her brother's bed. "Did you know she came here last night to find out how you were doing?"

Pete raised his eyebrows. "She did? No kidding?"

"No kidding. She stayed here for about an hour, until we heard that you were going to be all right."

"Wow. That's really cool. Tell her 'thank you' from me, okay?"

"Sure. I have to say, I was totally wrong about her. She's amazing."

Pete had a smirk on his face. "I hate to say 'I told you so,' but . . ."

"Okay," Traci said. "You were right about her, and I was wrong. You happy now?"

"Very happy," Pete said, leaning back against his pillows.

Traci stood up. "I'd better go to practice. Take it easy."

Pete laughed. "As if I had a choice here. Bye."

When Traci arrived at practice, Margo was waiting for her. "How is your brother?"

"He's doing fine," Traci replied. "He's coming home tomorrow, and he asked me to thank you for being there last night."

"I'm happy to hear he will recover fully. Now, I believe you have a lot of work to do to get ready for the exhibition. I'll talk to you about the dives you plan to do after you warm up. Be sure you do all your leg exercises."

And, just like that, Margo was back to being all business again. Traci smiled as she went into the locker room to change. Not long ago, this apparent lack of warmth on Margo's part would have made Traci furious. Now she knew better.

The group of divers with whom Traci worked did their stretching and exercising together, but each girl had an individually designed exercise routine aimed at dealing with her specific needs. Traci, for instance, needed to build up her leg strength. Carly spent more time on abdominal exercises, doing hundreds of stomach crunches a day.

After finishing her exercises, Traci got into her swimsuit and went to work on her dives. Margo watched each diver as she performed a dive and then took a few minutes to explain what the girl needed to do to improve. Traci began with a backward one-and-a-half somersault with one and a half twists in the tuck position. She knew that she had mistimed it even before she entered the water with a big splash, caused mostly by the backs of her legs.

Margo frowned as Traci climbed out of the pool.

"My come-out was too early," Traci said.

Margo nodded. "You need to work on your spotting and your head position. The two problems are related. When you left the board, your body was not in the right arch and you tried to correct it and over-compensated. You've done this better before. Let your body remember for you. Trust your body. This time, try a different entry, with your hands clasped. I think it looks better to some judges."

Traci listened and took it in. She waited for her next try, thinking about Margo's comments and about what had gone wrong the first time. When she re-peated the dive, she got the right arch in her back and remembered to change her entry as Margo had suggested. She felt in control and knew when to straighten out of the tuck. Her entry was much smoother.

Margo gave her a stiff nod of approval. "Remem-ber to flex your feet in your come-out. I think this dive should be on your list — the degree of difficulty is not very high, but you usually do it well. You might want to start with it to build your self-assurance and create a good first impression."

Traci said, "I was thinking of putting the inward one-and-a-half somersault with a twist on the list, too. How does that sound?"

Margo thought for a moment. "The degree of difficulty for that is 2.8. It's a hard dive. It's also a free-position dive — you can do it in the tuck, pike, or straight position. Which would you use?"

After a brief pause, Traci said, "Pike, I think. I've been doing it well."

"If you feel comfortable about it, it would be very impressive," Margo said. "Let me see you do it later."

"Okay," Traci said. She went to wait for her chance at the three-meter board and found herself next to Carly.

"I heard about your brother's accident," Carly said. "How is he doing?"

Traci filled Carly in on Pete's condition and added, "Margo showed up at the hospital and stayed until we knew that Pete was out of danger. I see what you mean about her."

"She's done that for other girls when they were in jams," said Carly, smiling. "But she's uncomfortable when people talk about it. She doesn't even know how to handle it when someone thanks her. The main thing is that, once she takes you into her world, she'll do whatever she can to help you out."

When Traci climbed up to the three-meter board

to try the inward one-and-a-half somersault with a twist, she went to the end of the board and stood with her back to the pool. Her heels hung off the board's edge. She closed her eyes and took a little extra time to visualize the dive. The key thing to remember, she felt, was to get a good jump. It was also crucial to really flex her abdominal muscles to get into the pike position and to give herself momentum for the somersault. Once she was rolling, Traci could then push forward with her right shoulder to start the twist. She should then be able to take her time in straightening her body into a line — the come-out — and to extend her arms for the entry.

But it was time to go. During a competition, even an exhibition like this, a diver was allowed only a limited time after getting on the board to complete a dive. If you went over the time limit, your score was a big, fat zero. Traci took a deep breath, bent her knees, swung her arms up, and jumped.

As she started the somersault, she looked for the clock that she used to spot herself and began to twist to her left. Her legs remained straight and her forehead touched her shins as she tumbled through the air and let her body stretch into a straight line. She tensed her muscles to hold that line and stretched her arms out to the side and then down. As Traci hit the water, she felt that she had done well.

Margo met her as she pulled herself out of the pool. "Be sure to flex your toes more and, whatever you do, don't wait too long before diving. You came close to the time limit on that attempt."

Traci sighed to herself.

"However," Margo went on, "this will be a good dive for the exhibition. You can score well on it. Now do a few more of them, to be more certain of it."

Traci knew from the coach's words, rather than from the expression on her face or any enthusiasm in her voice, that Margo was satisfied with her work. This meant that Traci herself had to feel very good about it, too.

Traci realized with a flutter of anticipation that she felt pretty ready to compete. She was eager for the day of the exhibition to arrive.

14

The day had come. Traci sat in the locker room reading her list of dives over and over. Her nerves were jangling and it was hard to sit still. Competition was nothing new to Traci — she'd been in lots of gymnastic meets — but that didn't mean she was any more relaxed than the other divers. There were eleven other girls who would be diving, some from Margo's class and some from the classes of two other coaches who had come to the center where Margo worked. All twelve were quiet.

Carly sat across from Traci, flexing and straightening her fingers. She stared at her hands as if she wasn't sure they'd do what she wanted them to. Carly had asked Margo if she could be in the exhibition although she had competed before, and Margo had agreed.

"I feel like a wreck," Traci whispered.

It seemed that Carly hadn't heard her. But finally the other girl looked up and managed a weak grin. "Welcome to the club."

"You too?" asked Traci. "I'm like, 'What if I fall off the board, what if I hurt myself, what if I'm so horrible I embarrass myself, my family, and the whole city.' Is that normal?"

"Pretty much," Carly said. "As far as I know, nobody has actually fallen off a board, but that won't stop you from worrying about it."

Traci was relieved to hear that she wasn't the only nervous diver. As she looked around at the other girls, they all appeared tense. One lay on the floor with her eyes closed. Another suddenly stood up and ran down the hall to where the bathroom was located.

Traci concentrated on breathing slowly and regularly. She focused on how she would do each dive. Unlike the daily routine of class, she'd have one shot at each; if she messed it up, the score she received would stand and there wouldn't be a chance to try again. Diving, Traci decided, was a very unforgiving sport.

Margo came into the locker room with a man Traci didn't recognize.

"Can I have your attention, please?" asked the coach.

The girls all looked up at her.

"First, welcome to all of you who are our guests today. Second, I would like to introduce Mr. Claude Duchair of the State Diving Association. He will run this exhibition and he wants to say a few words."

Mr. Duchair was an older man with gray, curly hair, whose posture and physique suggested that he might once have been a diver.

"Good afternoon," he said. "In a few minutes, we'll ask you to come out into the pool area and line up to be introduced. We'll also introduce our judges, all of whom have judged in many official competitions over the years."

Traci knew that there were five judges in most official competitions, except for national ones, where there were seven.

"Some official rules will be used today," Mr. Duchair went on. "Divers will be responsible for performing their dives in the order given on their lists. A diver performing the wrong dive will get a score of zero. Divers must perform a dive within a reasonable time after their names are announced. If necessary, a diver will receive a one-minute warning and must complete her dive during that time.

"Here is the order in which you will dive today. The order was chosen randomly."

He read off the names. Traci was eighth, and Carly was sixth.

"You have an eager audience waiting to cheer you on," said the official. "Take a minute to get ready, and then we'll ask you to line up in the order in which you'll be diving. Good luck!"

Traci's parents and Pete were in the audience with Valerie. Pete had been released from the hospital with a clean bill of health and had insisted that he was well enough to come. He had said, "I promise not to jump up and down and yell . . . too much."

The girls walked out and formed a line alongside the pool, to the applause and cheers of the people in the stands. Traci spotted her family and pointed them out to Carly, who showed Traci where her parents and sister sat.

"This is weird," Traci whispered as the girls were being introduced. "In gymnastics, you can make a little mistake without destroying your chances of winning. But here, a tiny little problem, and that's that."

Carly grinned. "*Right!* That's the challenge of diving! Isn't it great?"

She stepped forward and waved as her name was announced. A moment later, Traci did the same.

The first diver started up the three-meter board. She was going to try a back double somersault in the pike position. Traci watched the girl climb, position herself at the end of the board, pause, and hurtle into the air. She wasn't one of Margo's divers, and Traci thought she did pretty well, although her pike wasn't as good as some others Traci had seen. The judges awarded her scores of 6.8, 7.0, and 7.2. Traci joined everyone else in applauding. The diver's total score was determined by adding the three scores and multiplying the sum by the degree of difficulty: 2.3, resulting in a total of 48.3.

As other competitors did their dives, Traci moved closer to her turn, feeling more and more tense. The fifth diver did a forward double somersault in the tuck position and got very good scores: 7.6, 8.0, and 8.0. But the degree of difficulty was lower — 2.0 —

so her total score was lower than the first diver's had been: 47.2.

Now it was Carly's turn. Carly had chosen to start with a reverse double somersault, which meant that she would enter the water feetfirst. The degree of difficulty was 2.1. Traci thought that Carly had nailed it, entering the water like an arrow, with very little splash. The judges liked it, too; she got a 7.6, an 8.0, and an 8.2, for a total score of 49.98. Carly led all the competitors who had dived. But it was early.

Suddenly, as the next girl went up the ladder, Traci realized that she would be next. She tried to shut out everything else: the noise, the other girls, everything but her dive. She was starting with a relatively undemanding one: a forward one-and-a-half somersault with a twist. She'd do it in the pike position, and the degree of difficulty was 2.1. If she did it well, her score would be pretty solid, and, as Margo had suggested, she'd feel more assured.

She heard a roar from the crowd, meaning that the diver had completed her dive. She didn't even bother to look at the girl's scores. Over the loudspeaker, she heard, "The next entrant is Traci Winchell, trained by Margo Armstead."

Traci climbed toward the springboard. She was dimly aware that people were clapping, but as she got closer to the board, she forgot about the distractions.

By the time she walked out on the board, Traci heard and saw nothing but the board and the pool. She walked out to the point from which she would start her approach and closed her eyes. She still felt tense but was no longer aware of any fear.

In her mind's eye, she saw the dive as if it were on a video. First came the approach and hurdle, then the surging jump from the end of the board. Then followed the forward thrust to begin the somersault sequence. Her abdominal muscles would flex to bring her straight legs up until her forehead touched her shins. Then, once the somersault had started, her right shoulder would thrust forward to begin the full twist. She'd spot the clock when the full somersault and twist were done, then straighten out of the pike until her body was in a straight line, her arms stretched out toward the rapidly approaching water for the smooth straight-line entry.

Traci opened her eyes, focusing only on the physical tasks that she had to do. She started forward: the four steps of the approach and then the hurdle off her right leg. Then, after she came down, Traci flexed her knees and launched herself. Thanks to Margo's training, her legs were much stronger now than when she had started her diving months earlier.

Once in the air, Traci assumed the pike position as she began a somersault. She pushed her shoulder forward to begin the full twist. She saw the clock flash by and knew that it was time to start her come-out. The whole sequence seemed to be taking place in slow motion. She felt her body straighten out. She stretched her arms out to the sides and then overhead, clasping her hands together.

In the instant after Traci's hands came together, she hit the water. Immediately she flexed her fingers upward so that she would rise to the surface.

When she came up for air and swam to the side of the pool, Traci heard the applause and cheers. They startled her for a second; they were for *her*. For *her dive*.

She pulled herself out of the water and looked over to the judges' platform. The three judges held up signs: 7.4, 7.4, 7.6. A moment later, Mr. Duchair held up a sign with her total score: 47.04. Traci ranked fourth among the eight divers who had completed their first dives. There were still four more competitors, and four more rounds, so the exhibition had a long way to go.

She picked up her chamois from a bench by the pool and started to dry off. Looking up, Traci saw her family and Valerie, who were waving and clapping.

Traci smiled and waved back. She noticed Margo standing near the judges' platform. The coach gave one of her little nods. Traci felt great.

Then Traci forgot about her family and the crowd. She stopped thinking about Margo. In her mind, all that mattered now was the next dive on her list. She began going over the things she had to do in order to make it work.

Valerie was right. Whether Traci became a champion or not, she was going to give it all she had. As of now, she was a diver.

Matt Christopher

Kobe Bryant	*Michael Jordan*
Terrell Davis	*Lisa Leslie*
John Elway	*Tara Lipinski*
Julie Foudy	*Mark McGwire*
Jeff Gordon	*Greg Maddux*
Wayne Gretzky	*Hakeem Olajuwon*
Ken Griffey Jr.	*Alex Rodriguez*
Mia Hamm	*Briana Scurry*
Tony Hawk	*Sammy Sosa*
Grant Hill	*Tiger Woods*
Derek Jeter	*Steve Young*
Randy Johnson	

The #1 Sports Series for Kids

Read them all!

All available in paperback from Little, Brown and Company